ALL
TOGETHER
NOW

DICK, KERR GIRLS

ALL TOGETHER NOW

EVE AINSWORTH

With thanks to Gail Newsham,
official archivist of the Dick, Kerr Ladies football team.

Dick, Kerr Girls All Together Now is a uclanpublishing book

First published in Great Britain in 2022 by
uclanpublishing
University of Central Lancashire
Preston, PR1 2HE, UK

First published in the UK 2022

978-1912979-72-1

1 3 5 7 9 10 8 6 4 2

Set in 11.5/18pt Kingfisher by Amy Cooper

A CIP catalogue record for this book is available from the British Library.

Printed and bound in Great Britain by Clays Ltd, Elcograf S.p.A.

Dedicated to all the girls who have,
and who continue to push boundaries,
fight inequality and strive for more.
Empowered girls empower girls.

December 1920

1

The time was coming. I could hardly believe it.

I stared at myself in the dusty mirror that stood at the back of mine and my sister Hettie's bedroom. The glass was all smudged and there was a tiny crack that ran down the bottom left-hand corner, but I could still see my face well enough. I could make out my body, all bony and pale, as I stood awkwardly, one hand resting on my hip. I hoped Hettie was right, that I was getting taller. I had been making myself eat all of Mam's hearty dinners in the hope that I would grow quickly.

I pulled a face at my reflection, sticking out my tongue and crossing my eyes. I looked so daft, so young still. Was anyone going to take me seriously?

'Not if you keep acting like a ninny, Martha lass . . .' I muttered to myself. 'You'll have to stop this larking around and act more sensible, like Hettie. You need to be more like her.'

I straightened my features, pulled back my

shoulders and stared at myself again. Who would have thought it? Silly old Martha was going to get her time with the Dick, Kerr Girls football team. Maybe, at last, I could show everyone what I was capable of.

I was wearing Freddie's old shorts, the same ones that Hettie used to wear when she'd played for the Dick, Kerr Girls. They hung on me like deflated balloons. The bottoms were frayed and Mam'd had to stitch up a tear along the side, but they would still do me a turn.

The stripy top was oversized and swamped me like a shapeless tent. It was one of the girls' old ones. I didn't know whose, but I'd like to think it was one of the important players like Alice Kell or Flo Redford. Wouldn't that be a thing? Surely it would bring me luck! In all honesty, it was too old and tatty to be worn for games but was perfectly all right for me to wear at training. I stared down at the stripes, faded with wear. If I ever got to play a proper game, I would be given a little cap too. It would sit neatly on my head and finish off the look perfectly.

My legs were covered by huge dark socks, again, old ones of Freddie's; they itched against my skin and the rough darning felt uncomfortable and stiff against my toes, but at least they covered some of the bruises that were dotted across my legs. I wiggled to try and get used to the feeling.

I stood back a little and puffed out my chest.

Could I really do this? Could I really dare to believe that I could one day be a Dick, Kerr football player?

'You *can* do this, Martha,' I told myself, my voice strong and loud now. 'You know you can.'

After all, this was what I had wanted for so long.

It was an evening in early December, and I was outside on the street playing football again. I had to take advantage of every opportunity to get my practice in. I needed to get better if I was to be as good as the players in the Dick, Kerr team. I didn't dare turn up to training looking less than ready.

It was getting late, but I didn't care. I ignored the icy feeling in my battered boots; I refused to take notice of the deep ache in my legs as I moved. I was outside. I was playing. That was all that mattered.

And I had to win. I had to beat the boys.

'Martha! Martha! Over here!'

I moved across the cobbles, the ball stuck to my boot like it was glued. I only had to look up quickly, but I knew I'd left Davey on his backside. That lad was far too slow. Up ahead, Ronnie called again, waving his hands in the air, his face all puffed out and red. It made me want to giggle. He looked so daft.

I kept on moving. Our makeshift tin-can goalposts were within my reach. Feeling the bubble of excitement rise inside of me, I lofted the ball clear in the air, watching as it curled . . .

Would it make it?

My breath spilt out of me, leaving a whisper of smoke in the chilly air. I leant forward, my hands on my knees, my chest puffing hard.

The ball seemed to move at slow speed. The curl was almost perfect. I watched and waited as it drifted towards the target and then suddenly, stubbornly, struck the right-hand tin and rattled off behind for a goal kick.

'Martha!' Ronnie roared. 'You should've passed!'

I glared at him. 'I only just missed it, didn't I?'

'You still should've passed. You know that.' He glared back at me, his funny red face glowing. He swatted at his messy hair, his eyes blazing with frustration. 'It's not been the same. You've not been the same. Ever since . . .'

'Ever since what?'

'You know what,' he shot back, trudging over to collect his ball. 'Ever since you heard you'd be training with the Dick, Kerr Girls you think you're better than us.'

'I don't!' I shouted. 'But I can't help wanting to do well. I know I can be even better.'

He didn't even bother to turn round. 'You go on thinking like that, Martha,' he said. 'Go on. You're not even that good. Not really. I'm surprised your big head doesn't slow you right down.'

I charged after him. 'Why do you say that, Ronnie? Eh?'

Behind me, I could hear Davey, his breath catching, ragged in his throat. 'Hey! Don't be a daft apeth, Martha. Ronnie was only larking about.'

I shook my head. I could feel bubbles of rage spilling out of me, turning into hot sparks. 'I'll not have Ronnie talk like that about me. Just because he's as slow as a slug, he thinks he can say nasty things to me.' I paused, trying to keep my voice level. 'My head is *not* big.'

Ronnie snorted in response, which made me flinch with rage even more.

'Alfie's right about you!' he spat. 'You think you're so good.'

I glowered. Alfie wasn't here today – he was one of the older lads that joined in sometimes, but he had a nasty tongue. Everyone knew that he didn't like girls playing football. He didn't think it was right. I wouldn't mind, but the lad could barely kick the ball properly.

'Ronnie, don't anger her,' Davey whined. 'I don't want more arguments. This isn't fun any more.'

'It isn't fun playing with *Martha* any more. She won't pass, she bosses us about.' Ronnie kicked the ball over to me defiantly. 'Just because her family tell her she's some kind of football whizz doesn't mean she has to act like that around us.' He laughed loudly. 'She's only training with those girls because her sister works with them, that's all. And what's the big deal, anyway? Alfie says they're all talk and no talent. They're not a proper team.'

'That's not true! They *are* talented and Hettie says I could be just as good as any of them soon.'

'Not when you act all bossy.'

'I don't act like that.' I took the ball with my foot. 'I just want you to play the game properly, that's all. You still enjoy playing, don't you, Davey?'

I stared at Davey. I'd known the lad most of my life. We'd played football together as long as we could walk. Davey's head was bowed; it was like he couldn't bring himself to look at me. His sweaty hair was plastered against his brow. He swept it back and finally held my gaze.

'It's not like it used to be, Martha,' he said. 'You do boss us about. You shout, and you don't let us have a turn with the ball. You're always trying to dribble or do something fancy.'

'It's my ball,' I muttered sulkily.

'Well, maybe you should take your ball and play by yourself, then,' Davey said softly. 'I'm sorry, Martha, but Ronnie and Alfie are right. You . . . you think you're too good for us.'

With that, he gestured for Ronnie and the two moved back down the street – away from our makeshift goal and pitch.

Away from me.

Was Davey right? Was I really no fun?

I couldn't afford to be just a little bit good. I had to be *as* good, if not better, than the boys if I were to succeed.

I thumped the ball hard against the wall, trying

to control the frustration that was burning inside of me. I hated the fact my friends acted differently towards me now. It no longer felt the same, playing with them.

The lads were just jealous, that's all. They were just jealous of the fact that I was getting to train with the best women's football team in the country. Scrub that – the world! There were some folk now saying that the Dick, Kerr Girls were better than any men's team. So, stick that in your pipe, Davey! What would he know about it, anyway? How would someone like him get such a good opportunity as this?

I knew I was lucky. I knew it was the fact that my sister was close to the team that I got the opportunity to train with them. It also helped that Freddie, my brother, was their team photographer and was loved by the players as much as I loved him. If I was truly honest with myself, I knew I probably wasn't good enough yet to even be in the same training ground as these girls. But as Hettie kept reminding me, I had to keep practising. It was the only way I would get better and stronger.

I'd wanted this for so long, after all.

And then, one day, one wonderful day, maybe I too could play for the Dick, Kerr Girls.

I stayed outside, long after the lads had gone inside for their tea. I knew fair well Mam would be calling me in for mine soon. Freddie was already home from the newspaper and Dad had not long come back from the docks. I knew Hettie was having dinner with her boss, Mr Frankland, tonight, so we wouldn't be waiting for her. Even so, I hoped I wouldn't be called in too soon. I liked being outside, even when it was turning dark. The smoky scent of the evening air soothed me, and everything felt nicer, somehow. It was as if all the sharp edges of the day had been blurred away and softened. I always preferred being outside – it was so much better than being cooped up inside the house.

I still had the football – it was mine after all, or, Freddie's, if you wanted to be exact about it. The poor thing had seen better days and was rather battered, but I loved it. It was the ball that I had learnt to play with. Through this ball, I had found my first love – perhaps my only true love. I was reluctant to give it up. I had a weird feeling that I played better with this bashed-up thing at my feet. Perhaps it was my lucky charm.

I thundered the ball against the small wall that ran down the ginnel, liking the gentle feeling of the *thump, thump, thump,* as it rumbled through my body. I was pondering what Davey had said – it wasn't like him to be so mardy. Had I really changed that much?

The truth was, I felt like I had a lot to prove, being Hettie's sister. Although Hettie no longer played for the Dick, Kerr Girls, she had been a good player before being injured and now helped to manage and organise the team.

But I would never be as disciplined and controlled as Hettie, and Freddie always said I was 'the wild one'. Fast with my feet, but a little clumsy at times.

Me and Hettie were different in so many ways.

I just hoped I could be as good as my sister on the pitch.

Mam's voice shot through the air, calling me in. From the open door I could smell the scent of beef stew – rich and salty. Despite myself, my stomach growled.

Mam was looking at me strangely. Her eyes had that glint in them, which meant she was trying to study me, or even read my mind. She reached across the table and placed her hand on my chin, lifting it up to assess me further. I flinched under her tight hold. I hated being looked at like some pet in a shop. Her rough grip was really starting to pinch.

'Mam . . .' I complained.

'You've got a flushed face,' she said. 'Have you been getting into bother?'

'I was playing football out there. My face always gets red when I run.'

Mam sniffed. 'You stopped playing half an hour ago. I heard the lads' mam holler them in.'

I scowled – nothing got past Mam. She would make a grand policeman.

'I was still playing with the ball by myself, that's all.'

Dad laid his newspaper down and studied me for the first time. I noticed that his face had a grey sheen to it and his eyes looked small and dull. I guessed he hadn't slept well again. This was becoming the norm. I often heard him downstairs at night, moving around. Sometimes it kept me awake, too.

'Leave the lass alone,' he grumbled. 'You know she plays like a boy out there. She works hard, that's all.'

'Oh, I know that all right, but I know she quarrels with them too,' Mam replied. 'Only last week she got herself into a fight with that lad, Alfie, down the road.'

'He tackled me badly, I told you. He could have broken my ankle,' I said sourly. 'I only pushed him a bit. It's no more than he deserved.'

'And gave him a kick for good measure.' Mam's eyes fixed on me. 'He had quite a bruise on his side, according to his mam.'

'No doubt he deserved it. It's good the girl can look after herself.' Dad prodded at the paper. 'Especially reading everything that's going on. The world is changing. Martha needs to be strong. We can't continue to mollycoddle her.'

'I wouldn't say I do that . . .'

'Aye, well, I think we're all a bit guilty.' Dad's eyes glinted. 'She is our baby, after all.'

Mam sniffed, but dropped her hand, obviously satisfied.

Freddie nudged me.

'So, anyway, aren't you excited about your training sessions? They start soon, don't they?'

I nodded, my mouth chewing at my food, wondering

why it seemed so tasteless on my tongue. 'Aye. On Monday. I'm a bit nervous, to be honest.'

'You'll be grand, our kid,' Freddie said gently. 'Just remember what I told you before – listen well and keep your head.'

'I will. I just hope I can keep up with them. Hettie keeps telling me how quick they are.' I paused. 'I'm not as fast as Hettie was, you know? Or as strong.'

'I bet you will be, given time. You'll be as fit as a flea by Christmas.'

'There might not be Christmas for anyone,' Mam said shortly and then, seeing me and Freddie look up in surprise, she flapped her hand dismissively. 'I just meant . . . some ingredients are hard to get. Even now. And the cost of everything is going up.'

Dad shifted in his seat. 'I can ask for extra work. I told you that.'

'I can always get a job?' I added quickly, glancing over at Dad. Was it my imagination or was he looking thinner? How on earth could he take on more work? He was doing far too much already.

'You're still at school, Martha,' Freddie said, like I didn't know. 'You can't leave until you're fourteen. The rules have changed.'

'But if we need money I can fit in some hours after school or something? It's not like I want to be there anyway. It's a waste—'

'No.' Mam's voice was firm, cutting through my words. 'No. You don't need to do that, Martha. Freddie's wages are helping now. Hettie's too. We will be fine. School is important, we told you that. You need to focus on your studies.'

Dad nodded. 'You're only twelve, Martha. You're not expected to earn your keep just yet.'

I noticed he was moving his stew around his bowl slowly. Had his hand always been that gnarly? It reminded me of twisted tree bark.

'Are you all right, Dad?'

He lifted his head and his dark eyes fixed on mine. They were watery and made me think of chestnuts. He smiled, but it seemed pinched against his tired face.

'Aye, I'm grand, lass,' he said. 'But I'll be even grander if I know you're not getting into any bother outside. Can you promise me you won't?'

I thought of the boys – of their retreating backs and muttered words. I doubted I would be outside with them for a while. They probably wouldn't want to play with me again. A brief moment of sadness washed over me. Had I lost my friends for good?

'Martha,' Dad said, louder this time. 'Are you listening to me?'

'Yes, I am, Dad. I'm sorry.' I flashed him a weak smile. 'I promise I won't get into any bother.'

I just hoped I could stick to my promise.

2

Hettie and I were sitting in the bedroom together. Downstairs, I could hear the gentle hum of conversation between Mam, Dad and Freddie. They had been playing cards for a while; I think it had been Freddie's attempt to cheer the pair of them up. But now it was the simple sound of chatter and the occasional burst of laughter. I liked to hear that – it was familiar and comforting, like a lovely warm hug. I would be happy to wrap myself up in that sound for ever.

Hettie had not long been home from work. She had already had a wash and brushed her hair loose.

She sighed loudly and laid back on the bed.

'Oh, heck, Marth,' she groaned. 'I'm so tired. That factory was so busy today and then to have dinner at Mr Frankland's after . . . I don't feel like I've stopped for a breather. Mr Frankland wanted to natter on all night about plans for the girls – which was lovely of course – but I was so tired by the end, I could barely keep my eyes open.'

'That sounds hard,' I said. I knew how much I struggled to concentrate at school, especially when I was tired.

Hettie stretched out her legs. 'It was, but it was exciting, too. Mr Frankland was full of ideas about another charity match. We haven't been given much chance to prepare for it, but it sounds so wonderful. I think the girls will love it.'

'Really? What will it be?'

'Well, there's a local charity for ex-servicemen that are appealing for donations for Christmas. They have been speaking to the local councillors and all sorts. One of the councillors actually approached the War Office and asked if they could borrow their anti-aircraft searchlights—'

'Cor! It would mean you could play at night time!'

That did sound exciting.

'Exactly, and that never happens. Once again, the Dick, Kerr Girls will be the first to do something new,' Hettie said keenly. 'After all, why shouldn't matches be played in the evening? It makes perfect sense when you think about it. More people can come after a hard day at work. It'll be great fun.'

'It sounds it,' I replied. 'Who would the charity match be against? Do you know yet?'

'That's the most fantastic thing; Mr Frankland is talking about playing the girls against a team made up of the best players from the rest of England!'

'Wouldn't that be something,' I said, feeling a tiny stirring of jealousy. 'I wish I could be on the pitch with them all! How wonderful would that be?' I felt a flutter of excitement in my stomach at the thought.

'With the way the girls are playing at the moment, they should put on a grand performance,' Hettie added.

'Like at the St Helen's game?'

'Yes! Exactly.'

The Dick, Kerr Girls had recently played against St Helen's Ladies in Leicester. Over twenty thousand spectators had come to see their 4–0 victory, and all had walked away impressed at the skills on show. In fact, people were still talking about it now. People were still talking about it now.

'Well . . . it sounds like things really are very exciting right now,' I said, rubbing at my eyes.

Hettie sat up. 'You look a little pale tonight, Martha. Are you all right?'

'I'm just tired, that's all. I don't think I slept well last night.'

'Are you worried about the training? That's not like you!'

I forced a grin. 'I'm not really. I'm more excited.'

'Good. I thought you would be.' Hettie chuckled softly. 'You are so unlike me. I was a bag of nerves the first time I went to training.'

Hettie seemed so calm and confident now, it was strange to think of her as being nervous. I tried to remember when she had joined the Dick, Kerr Girls, but it was hard. They had only just formed a team. It seemed so long ago now. In fact, everything did. So much had happened in those three years – the war ending, Freddie coming home, the Dick, Kerr Girls rising to fame. So much had been squeezed into those years, it felt longer somehow.

'I didn't think you were that nervous,' I said. 'I remember you practising all the time.'

She nodded. 'Aye, I was shaking like a leaf the first few times I played properly with the girls. I never really had your confidence, Marth. It took me a while to believe in myself.'

Confidence? Was that what I had? I suppose

I was quite content with my football, but that was only because I had been playing out on the streets with the lads for so long and I knew I was better than any of them.

'I've asked Alice and Flo to keep an eye on you, anyway,' Hettie said. 'Those girls are so lovely and kind. They'll soon take you under their wing.'

'Thanks.'

'So, if training isn't the reason for you not sleeping, what is?' she asked. 'Is something troubling you, pet?'

I didn't answer straight away. Uncertainty nibbled at me. I didn't want to cause alarm.

'Martha!' Hettie insisted.

'Well . . . er . . . do you think Mam and Dad are all right?'

Hettie propped herself on her elbow. She frowned a little and pursed her lips together. 'Of course they are. They're the same as ever. Why on earth do you ask?'

'I don't know.' I shrugged. 'Mam just seems more worried lately. They both look so tired. I don't know, really. Something feels different.'

'You'd be tired if you had to sleep in the front room with Dad. Have you heard him snore?' Hettie smiled weakly. 'It's not right, us all squished up in a tiny house like sardines, especially now Mam and Dad are getting older. But what can we do? It is what it is.'

'Freddie says he will get a place of his own soon,' I said. 'I think he's looking at lodgings.'

'Aye, that he might, but he does struggle with his leg. He still cries out at night with his bad dreams too. Do you think many places will take him?' Hettie replied. 'It's a sad fact, Marth, but I think we will be like this for a while yet.'

'No wonder Mam looks so tired all the time,' I said, picking at a loose thread on my skirt. 'I don't want to be like that, Hettie. I never want to be like that.'

Hettie sat up further, her expression now solemn. 'Nor do I, lass,' she said. 'That's why I work hard. That's why I listen to everything Mr Frankland tells me. That's why I watch the Dick, Kerr Girls win their games in the hope that their light might spark something in me.' She chuckled softly to herself. 'After all, they keep telling me times are changing.'

'I want my life to change,' I said.

'And it will, if you work hard at it.' She patted my leg. 'And I know you of all people will work hard.'

The silence drifted between us. I watched as Hettie got up slowly from the bed, stretching out her body like a cat, kicking off her shoes so that they fell beneath the bed. Downstairs, the conversation still droned on. I could hear Dad's monotone voice, telling a tale of some sort. When I was younger, I used to curl up on his lap and listen to his stories all evening. But today, I just felt frozen on my bed.

'Hettie,' I said finally. She looked up expectantly, waiting. 'Hettie, do you think Dad's all right though?'

'Of course. Why do you say that?'

'He just seems different lately.'

'Different in what way?'

I shrugged again, struggling to find the words. Dad had always been tired; always looked in pain. How could I describe to her a funny feeling I had that wouldn't go away?

'Oh . . . I don't know . . .' I said finally. 'It's probably nothing.'

'You need to stop fretting, Marth. Everything is fine.' She smiled at me. Her lovely warm smile, that usually did everything to soothe me.

'Just concentrate on your football, lass,' she said, lying back down on the bed. 'I swear that team can change everything in your life. There's something about them. Something almost magical.'

I smiled back. I liked the sound of that.

My first training session was after school on Monday. It was a damp, cool afternoon and as I walked out of the school gates I already felt tired and fed up. The day had been a long one. Mrs Penny had been drumming the three Rs into our heads like we were babies and didn't know them all already. I thought it was daft that they were called the three Rs in the first place – reading, writing and arithmetic – when two of them didn't even start with that letter! Mrs Penny was also a health fanatic and, concerned about the recent cases of influenza in the area, had taken to flinging open the classroom windows to encourage fresh air into the room. As a result, sitting there in my thinning, threadbare uniform, I had spent most of the day feeling frozen and miserable.

And now, I was heading to the Deepdale training field to be put through my paces by the Dick, Kerr coach. I was still excited, but tiny doubts were trickling into my mind. Would I be up to the mark? Or would I just make a show of myself?

My body trembled at the thought. I couldn't let that happen.

Added to this were my worries about Dad. I had woken early that morning, unable to sleep, and had watched as Dad had left for the docks. I couldn't ignore how slow his walk was. How he groaned slightly as he stepped down from the door. How his chest seemed to be working hard as he made his way down the street.

He was becoming an old man in front of my eyes. And how come I was the only one who seemed to notice? Hettie and Freddie didn't seem worried at all. They probably thought I was just being a silly little girl, fretting about stuff that wasn't a concern.

They didn't realise that there was more to me than being a little girl who played football. I noticed things. I saw when things were changing.

That's the trouble with being the youngest in the family – everyone ignores what you say. They think you're the baby. When I told my worries to Freddie, he just ruffled my hair and talked to me as if I were daft. And as for Hettie – well, most of the time she just smiled and nodded at me like Mam would, placating me gently, like I was a child.

I puffed my chest out. I wasn't a child. I was twelve. I was growing up. People needed to take me seriously.

I walked briskly down the main street, down towards Deepdale, not wanting to be late. I pulled my coat tight against the sharp breeze. It was already getting dark. As I passed the terraces of houses, I could smell dinners being cooked and hear kids playing in the back yards. Everywhere, there was the sound of families settling and getting ready for their evening together.

I thought of Dad, trudging back from the docks. I wondered how much his back was hurting today. I hoped it wasn't too bad; that he could sit down in his favourite chair and take his mind off his worries. I'd come home and find him relaxed and happy, supping his tea and muttering about the state of the house – back to normal. I would be able to tell myself off for being silly. For worrying over nowt.

As I drew closer to the training ground, a tingle prickled down my spine. A horrible thought was bothering me, stabbing my brain in its nasty, intrusive way, refusing to let go.

What if I was right? What if there was something wrong with Dad? Something very bad?

What if everyone else was wrong not to listen to me?

I was a bit late arriving at the ground and the players were already warming up on the pitch. I hung back shyly, not quite sure what to do. Although I knew the girls fairly well from watching their games for so long, this felt different. I felt out of place here, like any moment someone would point at me and ask what on earth I was doing there.

I shook my head. I knew I was being daft, but even so, uncertainty rippled through me like a wave.

'Ey up, Martha!'

Flo Redford was jogging towards me, her bright smile welcoming.

'You came then, lass!' she said brightly. 'Hettie told us to look out for you. Are you excited? I know we are excited to have you join us.'

I shivered a little in anticipation. It was all I could do not to pinch myself. Was this really Flo Redford, one of the greatest forwards I'd ever seen, coming over to talk to silly old me? And she was excited about having me here. Who would have thought it!

'I am so excited,' I admitted, putting my school

bag down by the fence. 'But I'm a bit jittery too. My tummy is in bits. I feel like I will be wobbling all over the pitch.'

'Ah – that's only to be expected. You've got nowt to fret about, though. Everyone here is lovely. We all start off a bit nervous.' She leant in close and whispered under her breath, 'I had a dicky tummy when I first started playing. But don't tell the other girls, eh?'

I giggled. 'I won't!'

'We'll all look after you. After all, you're Hettie and Freddie's kid sister – that makes you part of our family already. Just try your best and I'm sure you'll be just grand.'

I nodded. That was certainly the plan. No one knew what I was capable of with the right training, not even me.

Freddie and Hettie already thought that I had pretty impressive skills, but that was on a cobbled street, wearing battered boots and an annoying skirt. Freddie had helped me to improve, working on my dribbling and such like, but he was at home less and less, now that the newspaper needed him here, there and everywhere to take photographs. I missed our time together, but I understood that his work was more important. Hettie couldn't help me, not with her dodgy knee, and now the lads on the street didn't want to play with me any more. But I would soon show those boys!

'You'd better get yourself out of that school skirt,' Flo said, pointing. 'Have you got some shorts?'

'Aye.' I pulled my skirt down, revealing my shorts underneath. 'I thought it'd be easier this way.'

Flo laughed. 'Well – it's good to see you're prepared, lass. When you've got your boots and that on, come and join us.'

I watched as Flo jogged neatly back to the others. Even in casual movement you could tell how graceful she was. I still had to shake myself a little. It was only a few months ago I had been in the stands cheering these women on. And now look at me – I was about to train with them. My dreams really were coming true.

I got ready hastily, tugging the oversized football shirt over my school shirt. I knew I would get a bit hot, but it was the best solution. I then pulled on Freddie's huge socks and boots, making sure I tied the laces tightly around my feet. As I jogged towards the group, my feet felt heavy and awkward and the cold wind whipped around my newly exposed legs, but I tried my best to ignore it. I knew I would soon warm up.

The girls greeted me merrily, slapping me on the back and squeezing my arm. Alice Kell took me to one side and told me to talk to her if I needed to.

'I'm always around if you need any advice,' she said. 'I'm a bit like a mother hen when it comes to new girls. Hettie will tell you the same.'

'Thank you. I'm sure I'll be needing lots of help.'

I scanned the faces, recognising them all, of course. My gaze finally fell on the girl standing behind the others. She seemed held back from the rest. She was standing a bit awkwardly and although she was smiling, she looked quite shy. I knew her at once as Lily Parr – one of Mr Frankland's quite recent signings and already a player who was making an impression on the pitch. In the games I had seen her play, she had certainly seemed to be the one to watch and I admired her greatly.

'She will be one of the best,' Hettie had told me. 'Mark my words. She's only young. Just a few years older than you, but her ability is second to none.'

In truth, that comment had smarted a little –

I had wondered whether Hettie meant that I was not as good as Lily and never would be. I knew now that wasn't fair of me – Hettie was never mean like that. But even so, I couldn't help but be a little in awe of Lily and also a little jealous.

What must it be like to have natural talent like Lily's?

We started off running up and down the track. Frustratingly, I found I couldn't keep up. My legs were useless and heavy in my clompy boots, and my chest felt pinched. I was nowhere as fit as I thought I was and felt embarrassed by the fact. As a result, I trailed the pack, coming in behind everyone else. I bent over, gathering my breath together in ugly gulps before raising my head and forcing a smile on my face. I didn't want the girls to see how disappointed I was to do so poorly. I wanted them to think I was still keen. However, I was angry at myself, wishing I could've performed better. If I kept this up, they would think I was useless, and they might ask me not to train with them again. My heart hurt at the sheer thought of this. I would have to start running more and improve my fitness levels.

'Never mind, lass,' Alice Kell said, trailing an arm loosely over my shoulder. She was glowing with sweat, having run as hard as anyone else. Girls like Alice never came last. She probably didn't know what it was like to do so.

'I'll do better next time,' I said, my breath still tight in my throat. 'I shouldn't have had that baked potato at lunch.' I could still feel it rattling around in my stomach. 'And I'll practise more, I promise.'

'Baked potato!' Flo Redford laughed. 'I remember having that at school. Baked in foil and always as heavy as lead. Every girl had to put their name on theirs so that it didn't get stolen. It always tasted so foul. All dry and hard.'

I nodded. 'Aye, it tastes awful, but you get a right telling-off if you don't finish it.' I rubbed my stomach. 'I can still feel it inside, like a dead weight.'

Alice laughed too. 'Ah, lass, no wonder you struggled a bit. I forgot you were still at school. I can't say I miss that much. The schoolmistress used to tell me off for kicking a ball in the yard.'

I smiled. 'Well, that's no surprise. Mrs Penny doesn't let us play either.' I paused and then lifted my head high, taking on Mrs Penny's pinched and snotty face. I put on a high-pitched voice.

'*Football is an undignified game, lass. Only foolish girls would partake in such violent and unbecoming matters.*'

Flo chuckled. 'Oh, I love the sound of Mrs Penny! What a card. I bet she would find me most "unbecoming".'

Mrs Penny didn't know I'd been wearing my shorts under my skirt all day. If she ever found out she'd probably have a heart attack, but not before giving me a good lashing. I just hoped she never noticed the rumpled creases around my middle.

'I wonder what Mrs Penny would have thought of us when we used to play at the factory,' Alice said. 'Do you remember, Flo? We used to play in long skirts – in the early days before we had proper games. It were harder, but we took those silly lads on. We beat them at many challenges. Your Hettie was there, Martha. She'll tell you all about it.'

'Oh, she has,' I replied brightly. 'She often says they were the best days ever.'

Alice nodded. 'Aye. It's such a shame she got that knee injury. She were an excellent player, you know.

Our old captain, Grace, said Hettie could've been one of the best.' Her eyes drifted to meet mine. Her gaze softened. 'Imagine if you have even half her skills . . . That would be something . . .'

I tried to smile back, but it suddenly felt stiff on my face. I was painfully aware that my breathing was still hard. That I was struggling to settle myself. I wanted to beat on my chest, wishing that I was fitter.

'Imagine . . .' I replied finally. 'That really would be grand.'

Alice nodded, seeming satisfied with my answer. She patted my shoulder and then moved away, her attention drawn to another girl's conversation.

I remained where I was, still catching my breath.

At that moment, I was happy just to be there.

At the end of the session the girls grouped together, talking, excited about their upcoming match. I hung back, a little unsure. After all, I wasn't a proper player yet. As I stood on the edge of the conversation, I felt awkward and small and suddenly very inexperienced. The football practice itself hadn't been as bad as the fitness training – I had at least had a chance to show my strength, which was in my dribbling skills.

I even managed to take the ball around Alice once, which drew some applause, although I did wonder privately whether she had just been nice to me.

I still ended the session feeling frustrated at myself. I hadn't done anything to stand out. I hadn't looked particularly impressive. I was nothing like my sister.

I was even less like Lily Parr.

Lily Parr had been the best player in training. She might be quiet in the group sessions, but when it came to football she was a different person. It was like something lit up inside in her – I swear she actually glowed. The other girls struggled to get the ball from her, she was that strong, and her shots – by heck! Her shooting had to be seen to be believed.

As if reading my mind, Lily appeared beside me as we walked back towards the gates. She was running her hand through her hair and smiling in my direction. She still seemed nervous, which seemed crazy. How could Lily Parr feel that way around me? That was impossible.

'By gum, that was tough,' I said brightly, feeling the sudden need to talk. 'I don't think my body has ever worked so hard. My muscles are complaining, I can tell you.'

Lily chuckled. 'Ah, you'll soon get used to it.'

'I'm Martha,' I said, holding out my hand. 'I don't think we've met yet, but I'm a huge fan of yours.'

Lily chuckled again. 'Oh, I remember you, pet. You were the one who curtseyed at me when I first joined the team.'

My cheeks were suddenly on fire. By heck, I had done that! How could I have been so daft? She must think I was such a silly little girl. I attempted to straighten myself up and pushed back my hair. I wanted Lily to see I was a bit older now, and much wiser.

'Oh, that . . .' I forced myself to sound confident. 'I'm sorry, that was a little silly of me.'

'Oh, no, don't say that! I thought it was very sweet.' Lily's smile was warm. 'It made me feel so welcome.'

'You're my inspiration. I want to be as fast as you one day, and as strong,' I replied. 'You were so good tonight. Just like you are on the pitch.'

Lily's cheeks immediately began to redden, and she turned her gaze away from me. 'That's good of you to say . . .' she said. 'I just do my best, that's all. Like all the girls. I'm nowt special.'

I opened my mouth to say more. I wanted to tell her

that she was wrong – that she obviously *was* special. There was something about Lily Parr that was different to every other girl I had seen play before. She was even better than the men that I had seen play. Fierce, fast and unafraid. Yet, Lily was like a different person walking beside me. She seemed more hesitant. She adjusted the hair that had fallen forward into her face and spoke again.

'I saw you today, too. I noticed how good you were with the ball. You just need to work on your fitness, that's all. Go out running. Get stronger.' She cleared her throat. 'I mean – that's what I would do if I were you. It'll help.'

'Thank you, Lily.' I grinned.

Her eyes met mine. I noticed for the first time how pretty they were – a warm brown – and as she held my stare, I felt a delicate shiver trickle down my back. It was as if someone's fingertips had just danced across my spine.

'That's all right.' She grinned, showing her white teeth. 'I'll always help you if you need it. Just . . . you know . . . ask. I've not been with the girls long myself, you know. I'm still finding my feet too.'

Still finding her feet? I nearly burst out laughing

as I peered down at Lily's tightly laced boots. I really didn't think she needed help with that! She probably had the best feet in the whole of the north ... If not the entire country!

'You seem to be doing all right,' I said instead.

Lily chuckled. 'I suppose I am. I just try my best. That's all we can ever do, isn't it.'

'I will try and get fitter,' I said thoughtfully. 'I don't like running much, but I suppose I can try.'

'I go cycling,' Lily said. 'I like getting out and about on my bike. It's great fun and it makes me strong, too.'

'Oh, that does sound nice . . .' The thought of cycling did sound far more pleasant than puffing up and down my street with the added humiliation of the lads laughing at me.

'You can come with me, if you like?' Lily offered. 'I could use the company. I often ride out into the country. It's so nice, even at this time of year. It helps to clear your head too.'

'It sounds lovely.'

'I'm planning a ride out this Sunday, if you fancy it?'

Her gaze fixed on me again and I found myself smiling back at her like a daft apeth. The chance to spend time with Lily Parr would be wonderful.

She seemed such good company, and maybe she could help me with my football even more. I mean, who could be better?

'I'd love to,' I replied keenly. 'If you really don't mind?'

'No, of course not. It will be fun. Let's meet outside the factory at midday. We can stop for lunch.'

It was only when Lily left that I realised that I didn't even have a chuffin' bike! How on earth was I going to be able to meet her now?

I spent the next evening staring forlornly at Freddie's bike. It was stood at the back of our yard. Its frame was all rusty, the front wheel buckled. I guessed the last time he used it was well before the war.

'I'm sorry, lass,' Freddie said as he stood behind me. 'I don't have much use for a bike any more.'

He glanced down briefly at his gammy leg, which had been injured during the Great War. I felt a shiver pass through me. I felt guilty for complaining. It was hardly Freddie's fault that he no longer used the thing. It was such a shame it had gone to waste, rotting away at the back of the yard. I'd never thought to use it before. I'd always been too busy out on the streets, playing football.

'Can it be fixed?' I asked hopefully.

'I doubt it, with that amount of rust. It's probably only good enough for scrap.'

'We should've oiled it for you – while you were away ...'

Freddie shrugged. 'It was old when I got it. Dad picked it up from one of the workers on the docks. I doubt it had much life in it anyway.'

I continued to stare sadly at the decayed metal, feeling disappointment wash over me. There was no way I could meet Lily now. Freddie's bike had been my last chance.

'Well – that's that then,' I said, a bit sourly.

'What was it? Why did you want it so badly?' Freddie asked. 'You've never shown any interest before.'

I shrugged. 'It were nothing really – just something I was looking to do, that's all. I'll have to cancel it now.'

'Are you all right, Martha?' His tone was gentle.

I looked up at him, noticing his kind face. I didn't want Freddie to feel bad about this, he had enough worries of his own. Instead, I flashed my brightest smile, the one I was used to putting on to make everyone else feel better. No one liked a glum Martha. They were used to me being bright and jolly.

'I'm fine, Fred,' I said, squeezing his arm. 'Let's go inside, eh? It's dead nippy out here. We'll catch our deaths.'

'Aye, let's get in the warmth.' He took my arm in his. 'And whatever it is troubling you, our kid, try not to let it get on top of you. Everything will work out just fine, I'm sure.'

Little did he know, the bike would be the least of my worries.

Friday soon approached and I knew there was something wrong as soon as I came home from school. I could sense a bad feeling when I walked through the door – a door that was wide open as I arrived, something that Mam never liked to do in the winter as it let all the cold in. The bad feeling grew as I stepped into the hall. It was like a heavy smoke, hanging in the air, whipping around me and slipping down my throat. My hackles were already up, and then I heard the soft voices in the living room. Mam's and one I didn't recognise at first – another woman's voice, slightly more formal, polite and stern.

I walked into the living room, clutching my satchel in front of me like some kind of protection.

The first thing I saw was Dad in his chair, which was wrong for a start – Dad was never normally home at this time. Then I noticed a woman standing to the right of him, leaning over and fiddling with his wrist. I realised it was Mrs Taylor, a neighbour from about ten doors down. She was a nurse at the hospital, and I knew that her and Mam sometimes talked in the street and exchanged recipes. Mam sometimes went to her if she had any medical worries. After all, we could never afford doctors' fees.

However, seeing Mrs Taylor here today made my skin prickle with fear. Mam and Dad never liked to bother anyone unless it was for something serious. Most of the time, Mam believed things could be cured at home with a hot toddy and a good rest. Seeing Mrs Taylor standing here, in our front room, her expression grave and her bag open on the table next to him, only made me feel more alarm.

What was happening?

Dad was facing away from me, his eyes half-closed, his mouth open as if he was struggling for breath. His skin looked odd. It was a strange grey colour with a sticky sheen all over it. It looked like he had been running hard and was now sweating. But Dad never ran. Not any more. Something was really not right here.

My stomach lurched. I turned round and saw Mam standing in the far corner. Her fingers were held to her lips. Her face looked ghostly pale. Her eyes were fixed on Dad.

I don't think any of them had even noticed that I had come into the room.

'What's happening?' I said, my voice breaking. 'Is Dad ill?'

Mrs Taylor coughed, dropping Dad's wrist back on his lap. She didn't bother to face me. Instead, she reached for her bag and began to rummage through it as she spoke.

'Your father had a nasty turn. I'm checking him over now.'

'A turn?' I blinked. 'What do you mean?'

It was as if Mam finally saw me. She snapped into action and hurried towards me, sweeping one arm around my shoulders and rushing me towards the door.

'We need to leave Mrs Taylor to her work now, Martha. She can't concentrate with you mithering on.'

'But, Mam . . .'

It was no use – she was already pushing me out of the door. Telling me to 'make myself useful' and put the kettle on, though I couldn't for the life of me think who'd want a cup of tea now. I certainly didn't. My stomach was swirling faster than waves on the sea.

If I drank anything now, I was sure to be sick. I only wished Freddie or Hettie were here too. They'd know what to do. They wouldn't be struck with fear like I was now.

As I walked towards the kitchen, I finally heard Dad speak. Surprisingly loud and forceful.

'I'll not be going to any hospital, I'll tell you that now. It's a waste of my hard-earned money. I'll deal with what I have to deal with here – in the comfort of my own bed.'

I closed the door to the kitchen and sank down on the nearest chair.

I shut my eyes.

I didn't want to hear any more words after that. I just wanted it all to go away.

A little later, I heard the front door close and then the hushed voices in the front room as Mam and Dad spoke. Dad's voice was louder, and quite forcibly he said, 'I'll not go there, love. I'm telling you. You'll not shove me in one of those hellholes to rot away . . . I'm not wasting our money on that.'

I busied myself making the tea like Mam asked, even though my hands were shaking. While I waited for the kettle to boil, I stared blankly out at the yard. I'd wanted to go out later, to practise hitting the ball against the back brick wall, but the thought of even touching the football was making me feel a bit sick. How could I concentrate now?

Dad wasn't well. I'd always suspected something was wrong, but this had to be bad, didn't it? Why else would he be fighting against going to hospital? I knew Dad didn't like hospitals, even if we *could* afford to go there. He always said they were 'where people went to die'. He couldn't even bring himself to visit Freddie when he'd been at the Moor Park military hospital. He said that the sight of injury and despair troubled him too much.

For a strong man, my dad certainly seemed to struggle with parts of life that others had to deal with. It was almost as though he found it easier to shut his eyes against the nastier bits of the world, rather than facing them head on.

The kettle whistled and the sound seemed to drill through my brain. I carefully poured out two cups of tea, trying not to spill the hot water over myself. The last thing we needed was Mrs Taylor back to attend to my scalds. I tried to push the scary thoughts right to the back of my mind where they couldn't bother me. And then I strode back into the front room with a huge smile painted on my face, acting once again like there was nothing wrong.

Happy Martha. Jolly Martha. The Martha that everyone loved.

'Tea's up,' I said brightly. 'Like you asked. I've made it good and strong.'

Mam blinked back at me then she smiled, but it didn't quite reach her eyes.

'Ta, lass,' she said gently. 'Pop it down there. There's nothing that a cup of tea won't fix, eh?'

I couldn't ignore how her voice broke on the final word.

Out in the yard, I tried hard to concentrate. The battered ball struck the wall sweetly and each time I caught it back on my foot, controlling it carefully with my boot. It was a skill Freddie had taught me. The longer I could do this for, the greater control I would gain in the game. Little things like this would help me.

I didn't notice the back gate open. I was only aware of Freddie when he came up behind me and lightly tapped me on the shoulder. He must have come home early from work.

'Oh . . .'

The sudden jolt made me lose focus and the ball spilled away from my foot and rolled across the yard. I scowled in frustration. 'That was my highest score yet, Freddie. Trust you to ruin it.'

'Sorry, our kid.'

Freddie perched on the doorstep, looking up at me with an amused expression on his face. 'It's good to see you practising so hard after school. It shows you care.'

'Of course I care,' I muttered, scuttling off to collect my rogue ball. 'Did you not think I did?'

Freddie shrugged. 'No, not that. You're just young, that's all. I thought you might lose interest. Or get distracted.'

My frown deepened. 'Well, that just shows what you know. The football is important to me. It . . . It . . .'

I trailed off. I wanted to say 'It is one of the few things I have left to enjoy', but something stopped me.

'What's up, lass?' he said quietly. 'It's not like you to be mardy like this, especially not about football.'

I shrugged, placing the ball back on the ground again. My foot trailed it lazily. How I would love to run with it now, just take off down the street like a wildcat, dribbling the ball. If it hadn't been so late, I might've been tempted.

'We have the big match to look forward to on Thursday night,' Freddie said in an almost coaxing tone. 'That'll be a grand one to watch, I'm sure. Hettie has been on about nowt else all week. You know that the local MPs have actually managed to borrow those searchlights so that the girls can play at night? I've never heard of such a thing.'

I nodded. 'It's quite amazing.'

'We are lucky to be going. I think it's going to be quite a sight,' Freddie said. 'I'll be writing all about it for the newspaper. My editor is very excited.'

I nodded again, my thoughts drifting.

'Martha?' Freddie's voice was more insistent. 'Are you sure nowt is wrong? Is it school? Or are those daft lads outside bothering you again?'

'No, it's nowt like that.' I paused. 'Didn't you see Mam and Dad when you came in?'

'Of course I did.'

'How were they?'

'Well – Mam is cooking dinner like always; she swatted my hide for trying to get a sneaky taste of it.'

He chuckled. 'And Dad was in the front room, I think. I thought he must have been having a nap so I didn't go in there.'

'He is sleeping,' I told him.

Freddie pulled a face. 'Well, I can't say I'm too surprised, Martha. He works hard down at the docks with men half his age. I dare say it wears him out. I don't think he sleeps well at night either. He has terrible trouble with his back, it keeps him up.'

'Mam had Mrs Taylor round,' I said flatly. 'She was here when I came home from school. They won't tell me anything. Mam says that Dad is just feeling under the weather.'

Freddie seemed to freeze. A frown creased across his face, but he appeared to push it away and shrugged slowly instead.

'And so? Perhaps he is? There's all sorts of bugs around. Gordon at the paper was poorly last week.'

I could feel my frustration rise.

'No, you don't understand. I heard Dad, Freddie. He was protesting. He was getting really angry – telling Mrs Taylor that he wasn't going to "any hospital".' I paused, realising that my voice had got much louder. 'They don't send you to hospital for just feeling under the weather. It has to be something more serious.'

Freddie didn't answer at first, but I noticed that he was gazing back towards the house. His forehead was creased again and his lips drawn together in a thin line.

'No,' he said finally. 'They don't. You're right.'

'What do think it could be? Do you think Dad is really ill?' I was wringing my hands now, trying to stop the shake. My insides felt like they were being squeezed tightly. It was difficult to breathe.

'I don't know, Martha, and that's the truth.'

Freddie shifted on the step and then beckoned me to join him. I huddled in next to him, liking the feel of his warm body next to mine. He was still so thin and bony from the war, but as his arm wrapped around me, I could feel his strength drawing into me. I hadn't realised, until then, how cold I felt. The evening air had a frosty bite to it and the skin on my arms was turning a grey-blue.

'It's too cold to be out here, really,' Freddie said, as if reading my mind. 'I'll help you practise at the weekend, if you like. Help you get stronger.'

I nodded. 'I just wanted to do something now . . . Take my mind off of Dad.'

Freddie sighed. 'Aye, I know. I understand, lass. I know Dad has been struggling with pain for a long time – maybe it's worse now. Maybe he just needs to rest more.'

'Do you think that's all? He just needs some rest?'

'I hope so, Martha,' Freddie replied. 'I really do.'

Thursday night was a bright and chilly evening, but windless and already fairly dark. Both Freddie and I were wrapped up warm in the Deepdale stands. Freddie was standing ready with his camera, and I was leaning over the railings, keen to get the first glimpse of the girls as they ran on to the pitch. I'd always done this since I'd first started watching the team play. Nothing had stopped the gentle thrill when I first saw them come out.

This was it. Here we go!

I'd never known excitement or fun like it before. It was like a warmth inside of me, a buzzing feeling of happiness that increased the more I saw of them. The Dick, Kerr Girls made me feel alive. There was nothing like it.

Looking around me, I couldn't believe the size of the crowd. Freddie reckoned that there were over ten thousand spectators, and the stands were heaving with wrapped-up bodies and faces glowing in a haze of breath. Everyone was so excited to be here. Down on the pitch, I could see the huge anti-aircraft searchlights placed on either side. They looked so strange and out of place.

'This'll be a great match,' Freddie said. 'I can't quite believe Mr Frankland managed to arrange it.'

'Me neither,' I replied.

Tonight, the girls would be playing a team made up of the best players from the rest of England. It really was a unique occasion. No wonder so many were here to witness it.

Not only were there lots of spectators, but there were lots of press too. I saw Freddie cast a doubtful eye at the large huddle of newspaper photographers gathered together behind the goal.

'Oh, look at them! They're interested now,' he muttered.

'Don't fret. I bet you still get the better photograph,' I assured him. 'After all – who knows the girls better than you?'

'But just look at their cameras. They are so expensive.' Freddie shook his head slowly. 'These fellas have come from all over the place.'

'Well, I suppose it just shows how important

the game is.' I paused. 'Is this the first to be played under light like this?'

Freddie frowned a little. 'I asked know-it-all Gordon at the office the exact same thing. Apparently, some professional men's teams have used them before, but it's never been very successful and never in front of so many people. I mean, just look . . .'

As if on cue, the searchlights were switched on, throwing their powerful beams across the entire pitch. It was quite beautiful.

'This,' Freddie whispered, 'is something else. It's the future.'

The game started promptly. To the crowd's amusement, the ball was painted bright white so that it could be spotted in the shadows of the corners more easily.

Both teams were fast and furious to begin with, but it was obvious that the glaring lights were taking some getting used to. I watched in frustration as one after another of the players became dazzled by them. This was made worse by the gaggle of photographers standing behind the goal taking photos.

'Bloody idiots,' Freddie hissed. 'If they keep

setting off their flashlights like that, they will blind the players.'

Unfortunately, he was to be proved right. At one point, Jennie Harris had the ball and was about to take a close range shot at goal. However, an over-enthusiastic photographer flashed his bulb at just the wrong time and Jennie managed to blast her shot clear over the crossbar.

'Oh no!' I cried. 'She will be so cross about that.'

Luckily, the girls seemed to adjust quickly to the new lighting. Jennie Harris, obviously fired-up from her previous mistake, managed to score two goals in the first half and, in the second, Flo Redford and Minnie Lyons each scored a goal of their own.

'Annie Hastie didn't have to make a save all evening,' I said to Freddie. 'What a result. 4–0!'

'It's as if they were born to play under lights,' Freddie replied.

I walked back home with Hettie, who had been down at pitchside with Mr Frankland, watching the entire game. Freddie had decided to go back to the office to develop his photographs. He was keen to get his to press before the others did!

Hettie was full of excitement as we walked back to the house, chatting about the fantastic game and how well the girls were doing. The girls had been invited as special guests to a supper, as a 'thank you'. Hettie had also been invited, but had called off as she felt too tired. She said this was the girls' time to celebrate.

'The Unemployed Ex-Servicemen will receive over six hundred pounds as a result of this game,' Hettie said. 'They are so pleased. They really need the money. The girls played their socks off tonight.'

'They always do,' I said. 'Jennie Harris was lightning-quick. She did well to score those two goals.'

'It's so funny that they kept losing her in the shadows tonight. She's so tiny, bless her.' Hettie laughed.

At one point in the match, the searchlights had gone off and the photographers had had to use their flashlights to find Jennie because she was so tiny and easy to lose.

'Isn't Lily Parr something else, too?' Hettie said, as we turned down our street. 'I can just tell she is going to be a fine player.'

'She's very quick,' I agreed. 'And so skilled with the ball. I don't think I've seen a boy play better.'

'Mr Frankland thinks she has the potential to be one of the best players ever – male or female,' Hettie said. 'That alone is exciting. Mr Frankland is a pretty good judge when it comes to things like that.' She paused. 'It'll be good for you to get to know her better, Marth. She's so close to you in age. She's quite a shy thing, but so funny with it. I think you two would get on very well.'

I smiled back wanly, not bothering to tell her that had been my plan all along. If Hettie heard that I had agreed to go on a bike trip with Lily, she might scold me for not being honest about not having a bike. Hettie always believed in honesty – she might not understand that I had just got a little bit carried away.

As we approached our house, I noticed that the lads were gathered outside.

'Here, look, the star player is back!' Davey shouted out, his eyes glinted in my direction. 'Don't give that one the ball – you'll never get it back.'

'Don't fret,' Alfie said loudly. 'We don't play with hoggers. Or girls, for that matter.'

I was dismayed to see Alfie back with the lads. He really was the biggest bully and loudmouth on the street and wasn't even a very good footballer.

'It's for the best, Martha,' Alfie added cruelly. 'You know you shouldn't be doing this anyway. Not if you want to be a proper lady.'

I could feel myself getting hot, my cheeks flushing with rage. There were so many things I wanted to shout back, but tears pinched at my eyes and the words seemed to be lodged in my throat like a giant boiled sweet.

'There's no need to be so mean,' Hettie shouted back at him instead. 'You're only jealous. That's all.'

Alfie simply scowled. 'You lot think you're better than us, just because you hang around with the Dick, Kerr Girls.' His face turned into an ugly sneer. 'They're not even a proper team – everyone knows it. Men's football is still the only proper sport.'

'Well – that's what you think,' Hettie said. 'Maybe you should come and watch them one day, before you make that daft kind of comment.'

Alfie was much taller, with mean eyes that seemed to pierce right through me and a nose that always appeared to be dribbling. He simply sniggered. 'You should enjoy it while you still can. My dad says there soon won't be a Dick, Kerr team. He's heard talk that important people will soon be stopping them.'

Hettie shook her head. 'Well, your dad is talking rubbish then.'

Alfie snorted. 'My dad knows lots of people. His brother works in London for a men's team down there. He's heard all sorts of talk.' He swiped the snot away from his nose. 'Lots of people are saying women shouldn't be playing football, not now that the men are back from war. What's the point? There are more important things for you to be doing, after all.'

'Like what?' Hettie hissed.

'Like staying at home and minding your own business,' Alfie replied. 'No girl should be out playing rough sport. My dad says your bodies aren't even designed for it.'

I could feel Hettie stiffen beside me. She made a clucking noise in her mouth. I knew she was gathering together an argument, but I couldn't see the point of continuing it out here. The likes of Alfie would never listen. It was like shouting into the wind.

I took Hettie's arm. 'Come on. Let's go inside. I've got no mind to listen to them blather on.'

Hettie frowned but moved with me, flashing an angry look back at the group of boys. 'I thought you were friends with those lads? How come they hang about with that nasty Alfie now?'

'Yeah, well, you thought wrong,' I replied stiffly. 'I guess things change.'

As we got to the door, I nudged Hettie gently.

'Do you think Alfie was right with what he was saying? Do you think there are important people that are trying to stop the Dick, Kerr Girls from playing?'

Hettie screwed up her face. 'Nah . . . I'm sure that daft beggar is just trying to wind us up, that's all. He's nowt but a big old windbag.'

I giggled at the thought. 'You don't think there's anything to worry about, then?'

'I don't think anything can stop the Dick, Kerr Girls now,' Hettie replied.

But there was something about the careful way she said the words and the way the tiny frown on her face lingered behind, that made me think she wasn't as confident as she was making out.

I could only hope I was wrong.

Inside, the house was very quiet. I could hear Mam moving around in the kitchen, preparing dinner.

Hettie went in to join her, to see if she could help. I decided instead to slip into the front room, to check on Dad.

He was sat up in the bed, the covers drawn close over him.

I walked towards him. His eyes had been closed, but they fluttered open on my approach. His skin still had a grey tinge to it and I could hear a faint rattle in his chest as he took his breath.

'Martha.' He reached out his hand. 'How was the game?'

'Aye, it were grand.'

'Good . . . Good . . .' He nodded, then tugged at his blanket. 'With any luck, I'll be up and out of here in no time. I can't be lying around, eh? Not when there's work to be done.'

'Mam says you need to recover.'

'Aye.' He swiped his mouth. 'I'll recover all right. I'll be back at the docks Monday. You'll see. Your mam fusses too much.'

I hesitated. I hated seeing my dad like this. I wasn't used to it at all. Normally, he was at work, or at the pub, or keeping himself busy around the house. I think I'd only ever seen him in bed once before and that was when I was a little girl and I'd had a bad dream.

My dad didn't belong in bed like this.

'What's wrong with you, Dad?' I whispered. 'Will you get better?'

'Ah, not much is wrong with me lass . . .' He fluttered his hand. 'That nurse woman says my heart is struggling a bit . . . bah . . .' He shook his head. 'What does she know, eh? I just need rest, that's all. And one of your mam's steamed puddings. Then I'll be right as rain.'

'You promise?' I asked. I felt like I was five years old again. My body was sinking, my head spinning.

'I promise, Marth,' he said, forcing out a grin. I could see his stained teeth, his fat tongue moving in his mouth. 'I promise, I'll be just fine. Everything will be back to normal in no time.'

Thump. Thump. Thump.

I continued blasting the football against the low side wall. I felt better being outside in the yard. I could still hear the shouts from the lads out on the street, but I had no mind to go and face them again. They would only put me in a worse mood. I didn't enjoy feeling like this. This wasn't me. I was usually the bright, happy, carefree one. Mam always used to say I could light up a room with my cheerful smile. But now it felt like I had the weight of the world resting on my shoulders.

Why was I feeling so glum? It wasn't just fretting about Dad. It was also the worry that I wasn't quite good enough to train with the Dick, Kerr Girls. This had been my dream for so long, but what if I couldn't meet their standards? What then? Would those daft lads on the street be right about me – that I was a silly girl who had got above herself?

Did they only include me because I was Hettie and Freddie's sister? I thought of Alice's kind face, of Flo's gentle words and I felt myself smart. I wanted to be there on my own merits, not because of any connections I had. Did this mean I had more to prove?

This was on top of the disappointment that I would no longer be able to go on the bike ride with Lily Parr. I planned to walk over to the factory tomorrow to explain to her, face to face. I expected that she would be very understanding, she seemed the type – but it didn't stop me wishing I could still go. What it would have been like to get out into the countryside for a few hours! To breathe in the fresh air and see different sights. All in the company of one of the most exciting players the team had ever had.

I shook my head, trying to remove the negative thoughts. My foot slammed the football again, harder this time. It bounced off, rolling along the far side of the yard.

No, enough of this. I couldn't afford to sink into this kind of thinking. It would do me no good. I needed to focus on the positives. I retrieved the ball from the other side of the yard. Then, more carefully this time, I began to play it against the wall again.

Thump.

I wouldn't give up. I would keep practising. I would prove myself.

Thump.

I might be Freddie and Hettie's sister, but I was still Martha. I could run rings around the lads outside. I was a good football player.

Thump.

It didn't matter if the daft lads no longer wanted to play with me. Who needed them, anyway? If they were going to listen to idiots like Alfie, they probably weren't worth my time.

Thump.

Alfie was talking nonsense before. The Dick, Kerr Girls weren't going to be stopped. Everyone could see how good they were. He and his stupid dad were just jealous, that was all.

Thump.

I didn't need to go cycling. I hadn't been on a bike for so long, I'd probably only make a show of myself. Maybe it was for the best. I would hate to show myself up in front of Lily.

Thump.

Dad would be all right. He would soon be back on his feet and as right as rain. All of this would soon be a distant memory. Something I could shove to the back of my mind and forget about.

I staggered back, my breath catching in my throat. I was building up quite a sweat and my legs were already started to ache, but at least my mind was beginning to clear. Like storm clouds passing overhead. I could now see my way forward. Everything would be fine, it always was. A smile settled on my lips.

I was so lost in thought, I didn't hear the footsteps behind me. Freddie made me jump as he laid his hand gently on my shoulder.

'All right, our kid,' he said, brightly. 'I see you've been working hard.'

'I've been at it for an hour now,' I told him. 'My control is getting much better and—'

I broke away mid-sentence. My attention was now taken by something standing just behind Freddie. Something that he had his other hand resting on.

'Fred – what is that?'

'Well, can't you tell, you ninny?' He laughed, pushing it forward. 'I'm pretty sure it's a bike.'

I stared at it in disbelief. Yes, it really was a bike – and a wonderful one at that. Its frame was freshly painted and the saddle was a bright red. Even better, there was a neat-looking basket attached to the front.

'Freddie!' I gasped. 'How did you get hold of this?'

'Well, you know the fella I work with at the newspaper – Gordon? Let's just say, he owed me a favour or two.'

I blinked at the bike in confusion. I had met Gordon a few times before – he was a large man, with a sweaty red face and a permanent scowl for an expression.

'Surely this isn't his?' I asked.

Freddie burst out laughing. 'Oh, aye! I could just see Gordon on this fine beast, dinging the bell and putting his papers in the basket. I'm not even sure his backside would fit on the seat.'

I giggled too. 'But you said . . .'

'I said Gordon owed me a favour. This belongs to his missus. She no longer uses it, so when Gordon heard I was on the lookout for a bike he offered it. I think he's still trying to make up for all the trouble he caused me when I first started at the paper.'

I frowned, remembering the stories Freddie had told me. Gordon hadn't liked it when Freddie joined the newspaper and even tried to stop him covering the Dick, Kerr games. I'd always thought he was a nasty piece of work. But this . . . this was lovely.

'Are you happy?' Freddie asked.

'Oh – more than you know!' I replied.

I swept him into a hug.

'Thank you. Thank you so much.'

5

Sunday couldn't come fast enough. I was so keen to go out on my bicycle and meet up with Lily. Of course, I had a few practice runs in the yard the day before. I'd never actually owned a bike of my own, but I'd sometimes had a go on Freddie's before it had got all old and neglected. I was a bit wobbly to begin with, but luckily it didn't take long for me to gain my balance. Gordon's wife had obviously kept the bike in good condition; it didn't have any squeaks or rattles.

Hettie watched me with an amused look on her face.

'I've never known you be interested in cycling before,' she said.

'It's good exercise. It'll get my legs good and strong.'

'Well, that's true enough. But what's this I hear about you meeting our Lily Parr for a cycle?' Her eyes glinted. 'It's got nowt to do with that, then?'

'A little.' I leant the bike against the wall and brushed myself down. 'I don't want to make a show of myself in front of front of her, do I? I need to get used to riding the thing.'

'You've certainly picked it up quick enough, but you need to be careful on the country roads. You'll be flying like a train down them.' Hettie pushed back a loose piece of her hair and seemed to be considering me for a moment or two. 'I have to say, I'm a bit jealous. You'll also get a chance to find out more about our Lily. She's such a quiet one, but interesting, too...'

'Interesting?'

'Well, she can be funny. Very sharp. And she seems to watch the other girls carefully, like she's really taking them in.' Hettie paused. 'She's young, like you, but somehow she seems so much older.'

'Oh...' I tried not to take offence at this. Was Hettie implying I was young in my behaviour? To be fair, Lily was three years older than me and had already left school – that seemed to make a big difference. I couldn't wait to leave school too, and for everyone to stop treating me like I was still a little girl.

'Any road – you should get to know her better. It's good to have friends on the team.' Hettie smiled. 'They become like sisters, really.'

I smiled back. I knew Hettie saw the team as extra family. I guessed it might help her when things were hard here at home. I looked over towards the house and thought of Mam and Dad inside. Freddie was out already, taking photographs for another game. I loved my family so much. I didn't feel the need for anyone else, and yet . . . It would be good to open up to other people. To have a friend to confide in. It wasn't as if I didn't have worries of my own; worries that I didn't like to trouble my family with.

I thought of my Dad, still sleeping inside the house. He told me was feeling better today, but was he just saying that to make me *feel better*? My head hurt just thinking about it.

I clambered back on to the bike.

'I'm going to have another go,' I said to Hettie. 'The worst thing would be to fall on my backside when I meet Lily tomorrow. What would she think, then!'

I woke up Sunday morning brimming, with anticipation. One quick look out of the window confirmed that the day was bright and clear. Thank goodness I wouldn't be riding in the rain.

At breakfast, I ate my porridge quickly, trying to

ignore the rippling feelings in my stomach. I wasn't really sure why I was so nervous. Perhaps I was still worried that I might make a fool of myself. If I was to do something daft, or even worse, be dull company, Lily might not want to see me again. My thoughts escalated. What then? Would Lily tell the other girls what awful company I had been? Would they no longer want me to train with them in the team?

Oh . . . I breathed out, sipping my tea and trying to steady my nerves. I was being a ninny. Why was I even letting myself think such things? I was hoping to chat to Freddie and Hettie, thinking that they might take my mind off things, but Freddie was still sleeping, and Hettie had already gone out to get some shopping for Mam. The house seemed strangely quiet.

'Are you all right, Martha?' Mam frowned at me across the table. 'You look odd.'

'I'm a little tired.' I swiped at my eyes to make the point. 'This morning's ride will wake me up.'

'Oh, that – you still on insist on going then.' Mam shook her head, but a tiny smile remained on her lips. 'Make sure you wrap up. Your legs will turn blue.'

'It's no worse than playing football, Mam.'

'No, I don't suppose it is.' Mam sipped at her own cup.

'Somehow, I seemed to have raised a family that insist on being outside in the cold all the time. They seem to prefer that to being inside this house . . .'

Her voice drifted. I saw something flicker behind her eyes. A sadness. My stomach rippled again.

'Mam . . . I can stay behind, if you like? Do you need help with Dad?'

Her head shot up quickly, like she had been slapped. 'Oh no, Martha – don't be daft. Go out. Get out of here. It'll do you good. I'm being a bit mardy, that's all. I don't need you here.'

'But I can—'

'Martha.' Her tone was sharp now. 'Go. Please. I'll be just fine.'

I slipped into the living room before leaving. Dad was sat in bed, propped up by pillows, reading yesterday's newspaper. He was dressed in his favourite worn white vest and shirt, and grey trousers. Although he smiled when I walked in, I could see how sunken his eyes were. He looked like he hadn't slept properly for weeks.

'I'm going out for a bit,' I told him. 'Do you want me to fetch you anything?'

'Sunshine?' Dad joked, and then started coughing

as the idea seemed to overwhelm him. 'Sorry, lass, I'm just being daft. Being stuck indoors all day is sending me barmy.'

'How are you feeling?'

'I'll be all right. I'll be back at the docks tomorrow. I can't sit around here on my backside all day.' He shifted in the bed, as if to make the point.

I stepped back a little, confused. 'But Dad, aren't you still . . .' I paused, flustered. 'Mam said you were to rest.'

Dad flapped his hand at me. 'Aye, your mam says a lot of things. Most of them nonsense. A man has to work, Martha. He does no good idling around and getting in the way.'

'But you need to get better.'

'There's nowt wrong with me.' He sat up straighter. 'Nowt wrong at all. I can't be doing with all this fussing. It makes my head ache. Now, aren't you meant to be off out somewhere?'

I shifted on the spot. I needed to leave soon – I didn't want to be late for Lily – but there was an invisible thread pulling me towards Dad. I could see something in Dad's eyes that I had never seen before. There was a sadness – a vulnerability that didn't belong there.

This was my dad. My big strong dad, and yet now, he looked small.

Tired and small.

And I hated it so much. It made me ache inside.

'Dad . . .' I whispered. 'I'm worried.'

His large hand reached out and took mine. The grip was still strong. I stared down at his skin, stained dark by his outside work and so rough to touch. His veins bulging out like grey worms.

'I'm fine, lass,' he said. 'I told you. I'm fine. Now go. Go outside and have some fun. I don't like to see you so serious.'

He released his grip and sank back into the pillows. The last thing I saw as I left the room was his tired face as he turned it away from mine.

I set off on the bike, still quite wobbly, down the cobbled street towards the factory. I was pleased that the lads weren't out playing yet. I wasn't sure I could face their heckles this morning. Only Alfie was about, sitting on his wall, kicking his feet against the bricks. He flashed me a bemused look as I cycled past.

'Ey up, Marth. Got yourself some wheels now?' he called out. 'Watch you don't tumble on the cobbles;

you might bang some sense into that daft head of yours!'

I ignored him, even though he continued to jeer as I wobbled past. I wondered what was wrong with that boy and why he insisted on being so nasty to me. What had I ever done to him? Was he really that bothered by the fact I was better than him at football?

I continued my journey towards the Dick, Kerr factory, trying to clear my mind of that daft lad. On my shoulder, I had a bag stuffed with cheese sandwiches that Mam had packed and a bottle of pop that Freddie had given me. It was quite a heavy load!

'Martha!'

I looked up and saw that Lily was already waiting by the factory gates. Her bike was leaning up against the gate itself and she was munching on an apple. She swiped her hand over her mouth and tossed the apple core into a nearby bush.

'What kept you?' she asked. 'I thought you'd been run over by a tram.'

'I . . .'

I really wasn't sure what to say. Was she angry with me?

But then she laughed, and I immediately relaxed.

'I'm only kidding, lass. Come on, shall we make a move while the sun's still shining?'

And just like that, Lily Parr and I were off – down the main streets and out into the countryside. Just me and her.

On an adventure of our own.

We stopped amongst fields that stretched out beyond Preston. My legs were aching badly, and my lungs felt like I'd played sixteen football matches on the trot. I didn't want Lily to think that I was weak, so I didn't say anything. I just hoped she didn't notice how red-faced I was, or how much I was struggling to get my breath. The hills had been the worst. Lily'd had to check back a few times to make sure I was all right. I kept blaming the 'old bike' for the reason I was wobbling, and not the fact that I was out of practice. I wasn't sure she believed me, but she didn't say anything.

I was glad to get off the bike, my legs were aching a treat! I tried to disguise my discomfort as I staggered next to Lily.

'You all right, lass?'

'Oh, yes.' I puffed out my chest. 'That was right good. I feel much better for it.'

Today, I wanted to show her that I was grown up and interesting – not babyish and annoying.

Lily spread out her coat so that we could sit down on the damp grass. Luckily, the sun was shining, and the exercise had warmed us up enough that we didn't mind the chill of the breeze. She unzipped her large bag and pulled out a thick wad of sandwiches and a big bag of crisps.

'Everyone always jokes I have the appetite of a horse,' she said plainly, tucking in. 'It drives Alice mad. She says I eat her out of house and home.'

'Alice?'

'Alice Norris.' Lily looked at me as if I was a bit daft. 'Don't you know that I live with her and her family? I moved in when I joined the team. It made it a lot easier for me.'

'Oh no, I didn't know that . . .' I nibbled at my own sandwich, thinking this over. I knew Hettie had told me that Lily and Alice were close friends. Maybe she had told me that Lily was living there too. I didn't always listen to everything she said – I got easily distracted. It was no wonder that I was confused at times!

'It must be nice, living in the same house as Alice,'

I mused. I would like that – to live with a friend. I stole a shy peek at Lily and tried to imagine what it must be like to live with her. I decided it would be fun. A tiny spark ignited inside of me and I realised that I was jealous of Alice. How lucky she was to spend so much time with Lily.

'Aye, it's grand,' Lily said, munching on her food. 'But we've had a few words.' Her eyes glinted with mischief. 'I think she's getting used to my ways.'

'Oh, really? How's that?'

'Well – I was meant to share a room with her, but I wasn't having that,' Lily said, matter-of-factly. 'I like my own space. I told Alice she'd have to sleep somewhere else.' She looked a little embarrassed. 'I did tell her nicely, mind.'

'You chucked her out of her own bedroom?' I replied, shocked.

Lily grinned. 'Well, it wasn't as bad as that. Her mam got her a new bed and everything. Even Alice admitted it worked out well in the end. She really wouldn't really want to share a room with me. I'm a right pain – honestly. And I like my own space too much.'

I thought of my crowded room back at home, stuffed into the same space as Freddie and Hettie.

Most of the time it was fine, and I didn't even think to complain. But there were times, when I was tired or feeling a little weary, when I longed for my own space. Some place to be where I could think my thoughts, uninterrupted.

'It's so busy at mine,' I said. 'All the comings and goings. Sometimes it makes my head spin.'

'Oh, my house used to be like that,' Lily replied. 'When I go back to see my mam I'm reminded of how chaotic it is. My mam – she is the best . . .'

Her voice broke a little. She stopped eating.

'You must miss her.'

'Aye, I do. I still see her lots, but we're close, my mam and me. She really understands me, I suppose.'

I nodded. 'My mam is a bit like that. Although I suppose, in truth, I'm closer to my dad.'

My voice wobbled a bit. I didn't like to talk about him, not with the way he was. It made my worries about him come tumbling back to the front of my mind.

'That's nice though. Is he happy that you play football?' Lily asked. 'I know some folks aren't. Especially the men.'

I shrugged. 'He wasn't at first. He does have some old-fashioned ways. Poor Hettie got the brunt of it when she was playing. But I think he's softened a bit. I think . . . well, I guess his priorities are changing. Other things bother him more now . . .'

I blinked and looked away. I could feel that nasty, twisty sensation in my stomach again. Like a hole was opening up inside it and letting icy air in.

She looked at me, her gaze was soft. 'Are you all right, Martha?'

I managed a tight smile. I didn't want her to know that I was getting upset and that my silly tears were threatening to spill.

What was wrong with me? I was turning into a cry baby, in front of Lily, of all people.

'Oh, I'm all right. Don't worry about me. I've just got lots on my mind.'

'I know what that's like.'

'I guess that's why I love football so much,' I said quietly. 'As I said, I don't really have my own space, but when I'm out practising with my ball, it's different. I can . . . well, I don't know . . .'

I hesitated, suddenly feeling daft. I could feel Lily's eyes on me, and my skin felt hot, like her gaze was burning into me. I felt like she could see right inside me.

'Oh, I do know . . .' she said softly. 'I totally know what you mean, Martha. Sometimes I think I'm most alive when I have the ball at my feet. Normally, I'm happy being the quiet one. In the shadows, watching others and the like.' She paused; her gaze had drifted now. She seemed to be staring off somewhere in the distance. 'But when I'm playing football, it's as if I'm a different person. It's hard to explain really. It's like I've been lit up from inside. I feel so . . .'

'Free?' I offered.

'Yes!' She slapped my shoulder. 'Yes, Martha, that's it! I feel free. And so happy. Football gives that to me. It's so special, but so hard to describe.'

I grinned. I understood completely what she meant. Football brought out all those emotions in me too. Since I was a little girl, it had made me happy.

But as I sat with Lily now, so close to her that I could touch the soft skin on her leg and feel her gentle breath on my neck – another realisation had struck me.

Lily liked me!

Since the lads had left me, I had felt a little bit abandoned and out of sorts, but now I was sat next to this wonderful girl. A girl who was the same as me in many ways. We had so much in common!

Could I dare believe that a girl like Lily might become my friend?

6

As we fast approached Christmas, I found that I was struggling more and more to concentrate at school. More often than not, Mrs Penny would rap my knuckles with a ruler or make me stand in the corner of the class – telling me off for being 'away with the fairies'. Mrs Penny didn't understand. I had more to worry about than daft arithmetic and spellings. The training sessions at Deepdale were getting harder and harder and I was struggling a bit to keep on top of it. I was also fretting about my dad. He'd only just gone back to work. He'd also lost a lot of weight and was moving at half the speed. His shoulders were slumped in such a way it looked like he was carrying a huge weight upon them. It broke my heart in two to see him like that.

I hated school even more than usual. I struggled to sit still with a nice straight back like the other girls. I kept turning my head towards the window, gazing out at the fields beyond. All I wanted was to be outside. Either playing football or watching it. School seemed like such a waste to me now.

'Martha!' Mrs Penny snapped again, her ruler clasped firmly in her fat hands. 'Eyes to the front!'

I sighed softly.

I was twelve now. In two years, school would be over. Just two years.

But what then?

What would I do with myself?

'You could work at the Dick, Kerr factory, like your sister and the other lasses?'

I was putting on my boots at the side of the field at the start of training. Lily was already stretching next to me, keen to get started. I'd just been telling her my worries, wondering out loud what I would do when school was over.

'Factory work isn't so bad,' she added kindly. 'It's busy and it makes you stronger.'

'Perhaps.' I tightened my laces. 'I'm not sure. There's not so many jobs now, are there?'

Hettie had been complaining about this recently. Now that the war was over, many women, who had previously been doing the physical tasks that the men had been doing, had been laid off. Women were no longer needed as much. I knew that the brighter girls in school would train to be secretaries or work in offices in town – but I wasn't like them. I would soon get bored in a job like that, and I wasn't exactly the brightest spark in class.

'There's no hurry, is there?' Lily said, looking at me curiously. 'You have time.'

'I do . . .' I replied. 'I suppose . . .'

Except it didn't really feel like it; time seemed to be slipping away from me like sand through my fingers. I wasn't sure how long Dad would be able to keep working. Freddie was looking to move away soon and get a place of his own, and who could blame him? It couldn't be easy sharing a bedroom with two sisters. If he left, then Mam might be relying on Hettie's money alone, and I knew she didn't earn much. She often grumbled that she was paid half of what the men earnt, even though she worked just as hard.

Lily smiled awkwardly. 'It'll be all right, lass. Chin up, eh? Let's go and join the others. A run around will do you the world of good and take your mind off things.'

'Aye, you're right. I just wish my legs didn't feel like lead.'

'That'll soon wear off.'

I ran alongside her, fixing my smile back on my face and making the best of it.

I might not be as good as the rest of the Dick, Kerr Girls, but I was going to have a jolly good go at keeping up for as long as I could.

Today's session was still hard work, but a little bit different. The coach had us playing a game of leapfrog. We lined up and raced against one another. I was partnered with Lily, which I was thankful for as she was so fast. I had never considered this game to be particularly hard work, but then again, I'd only ever played it out on the streets for larks. In training it was much more competitive, with our coach ordering us to go faster and faster. It was the first time I'd ever really had such fun in training and I clearly wasn't alone. Most of us ended up on our backsides, crying with laughter!

'We're doing some boxing next week,' our coach told us all at the end. 'And perhaps some skipping, too.'

'That'll be fun,' Alice said keenly.

'Boxing?' Flo looked shocked. 'I'm not sure I'd be much good at that.'

'You will, lass,' Alice assured her. 'These exercises are to help us become nimble and able to play a fast game on a heavy pitch.'

'And who doesn't love a game of leapfrog!' Lily added.

The girls roared with approval.

'We can work hard and enjoy ourselves at the same time,' Alice agreed. 'After all, that's what the Dick, Kerr Girls do best.'

Back at home, Hettie was full of excited chatter about the upcoming Boxing Day match, which was only a week away. She had already secured me and Freddie tickets to watch. This was always the highlight of our Christmas, watching the girls play – and by all accounts, this was going to be the best game yet. Unlike other games, where we had simply walked across the street to Deepdale, this time we would be travelling far further afield – to Liverpool and the home of Everton at Goodison Park. The Dick, Kerr Girls would be playing their close rivals and fellow superior girls' team, St Helen's, from Lily's home town.

'I still can't believe the girls will be playing there,' Hettie said. 'Can you imagine? Ladies' football taking place at one of the biggest and best pitches in Merseyside. It's going to be quite a sight.'

Freddie nodded. 'Everyone at the newspaper is excited, too. This really will put the girls on the map.'

'Mr Frankland can't stop talking about it. He's been bouncing around the factory like a little boy.' Hettie giggled. 'He's really pleased they will be playing St Helen's again. The last match was so impressive.'

There had been a recent game that I hadn't attended, but Hettie had told me it had drawn a crowd of over twenty-two thousand fans. People were coming from far and wide to watch these teams play. Hettie had shown me a scrapbook that Mr Frankland was keeping of the Dick, Kerr Girls' achievements. In it he had written:

It's coincidental to think that in leading the way among ladies' teams of the land, Dick, Kerr's are but emulating what 'Proud Preston' did in men's football way back in the 1880s. Preston North End were known then as the The 'Invincibles': Dick, Kerr Ladies are the invincibles today.

It was so lovely to see how proud of his team Mr Frankland was, and how much he obviously believed in them.

'Mr Frankland thinks that Goodison is the perfect ground for the girls to play on, especially now they are attracting such huge crowds,' Hettie said. 'This is where they deserve to be.'

'I don't think anyone doubts it,' I replied.

'Oh, I'm not sure about that,' Freddie said softly. 'There's still those that are saying the women shouldn't be entertaining such things . . .'

Hettie scoffed. 'What people? Why are they still continuing these daft arguments?'

'Don't ask me, it makes no sense.' Freddie shrugged. 'But there's still folk grumbling in the office and I've heard talk on the pitchside too. There's those that have read the articles in the newspapers. Have you seen them? There are all sorts of people complaining. The government and doctors coming out and saying that women shouldn't be playing sport – that it's not good for them.'

Hettie sniffed. 'I've never heard of anything so daft! How can sport be bad for you?'

'Mrs Penny said that it's unnatural,' I said quietly,

remembering an occasion when she had taken me aside before training. Her body all stiff and tense, her face pinched with concern. One of the girls at school had told her what I had been doing on a Monday evening and she wasn't happy about it at all. 'She told me that God never intended for women to be running up and down football pitches. She said I could do myself a mischief.'

Freddie laughed out loud. 'Well, I suppose it's nice she's showing such a concern.'

'Is it heck as like!' Hettie replied. 'What does she think our bodies are for? Just cooking and cleaning and rearing babies? I can't believe we are still having these same arguments. The suffragettes fought for us against this nonsense. Things are meant to be improving – and yet . . .' She shook her head slowly. 'I don't know. Sometimes it just seems like we go two steps forward and five steps back. The girls are doing so well now. The games are getting bigger and bigger. I hear the fans talking afterwards; they are so excited – they love watching the girls play. Mr Frankland has such wonderful plans. There's talk of the team travelling to other countries, playing new teams. This should be the time for celebration.'

'And it still is,' I said. 'You've heard this all before, Hettie. Why are you letting it bother you now?'

She shook her head. Her face was pale now. I noticed she was chewing on the inside of her cheek, something she always did when she was anxious or thinking something through.

'I dunno, Marth. I just have a bad feeling, that's all. I don't like it. I don't understand why so many are speaking out against the girls.'

'Perhaps they are jealous, I mean – their games are getting so popular. Some might say they are just as popular as the men now,' I said, thinking of Alfie down the road and his hatred towards girls playing football.

'And so they should. They are just as good!' Hettie said.

Freddie nodded. 'And I agree. But there are many that don't see it that way . . .' He paused. 'Marth is right. There are many people out there that won't be happy to see the men's game pushed out of the limelight. They will do whatever they can to make sure that doesn't happen.'

Hettie grumbled softly under her breath, but I could see her eyes were as hard as flint.

'They won't stop us,' she said finally. 'They can

try if they like, but nothing is going to stop the Dick, Kerr Girls now.'

Later, I was out in the street. It was dark. Too dark to practise football, so I just sat in the early evening night, my coat pulled tightly around me, drinking in the sharp, cool air.

Inside, Freddie and Hettie were in our bedroom. Hettie was reading and Freddie was writing a letter to his old army friend, Micky. Both of them wanted to be quiet. No one wanted to talk. Mam was preparing dinner. Usually, I'd help her, but she had sent me away, complaining that I was getting under her feet. I think Mam had a lot on her mind too. Her face seemed constantly etched with a frown and she kept checking the door, waiting for Dad to arrive home.

We both knew he was late.

I watched the street earnestly. It was quiet tonight, hardly anyone was about. I felt so cold and numb just sitting there, I even started to question why I was doing it.

You're so daft, Martha. What are you expecting, eh? To see your dad coming home all merry and bright? Perhaps he's been down the pub? He hasn't been to the pub for so long, but it would explain why he's late. The pub would cheer him up for sure. That would be a sign that he was getting back to his old self . . .

Finally, I saw him. However, it wasn't the unsteady movements of someone that had been out enjoying himself. The person moving towards me looked like an old man. He was moving more slowly than he had before. His body appeared crumpled, as if bent back by the wind; his head was lowered towards the cobblestones.

'Dad . . .' I got up, moved towards him.

He looked up, blinking in the poor light. 'Martha? What are you doing out here? You'll catch your death!'

I hadn't noticed before, but Dad's coat was so thin and worn in places. There was a hole in one arm; I could see his pale skin. Now I was closer, I peered up at his face. In the dim light I could see that his eyes were weary.

'You need to get inside, Dad. You look tired,' I said.

'Aye.' He sighed, and it rippled through his entire body. 'It's been a long day.'

'You were late. I was starting to worry.'

His hand rested briefly on my shoulder. 'Martha. You always worry about others. You're such a good girl. I'm sorry if I worried you. Work just took longer today, that's all.'

We walked into the house together, greeted by the comforting smell of Mam's homecooked pie. It was Dad's favourite. I turned to him, smiling.

'You're back now. That's all that matters.'

He nodded. 'Aye, you're right, that's all that matters.'

There was something in him, a sadness, that rippled through me and made me want to cry out loud. But as usual, I simply pushed that thought to the back of my mind.

After all, what was the use of worrying? I had to keep telling myself that everything would be just fine.

It was here! The run up to Christmas had flown by in a heartbeat. For once I was barely interested in the gifts I'd received on Christmas Day (a book and new blue dress) or even had much care to eat the dinner that Mam had prepared. I was far too excited for the game at Goodison Park.

The morning of Boxing Day passed in a flurry of excitement. I could barely stand to eat any of my breakfast, despite much nagging from Mam. Even my worries about Dad were pushed further to the back of my mind. I kept telling myself that he would be all right. He was my dad after all. My big strong dad. He always came through all right in the end and worrying and fussing about him wouldn't help at all.

So, today, I allowed myself to feel excited. Even Mam was caught up in the flurry of activity as Hettie, Freddie and I got ready to leave – moving from room to room, looking for our boots, jumpers and scarves and talking loudly in energetic chatter.

'Honestly! Anyone would think you were meeting the king, the way you lot are acting!' Mam laughed, throwing her arms in the air. 'I've never seen you all so merry.'

'Oh, this is far better than meeting the king,' Hettie replied. 'Mam – this game will be huge. Mr Frankland says that there might be as many as thirty thousand people there. Maybe more!'

'I know,' Freddie said keenly. 'It will be the best one I've covered for the paper yet. Mr Jackson will be pleased.'

He was busy getting his camera equipment together – there was so much of it, I often felt sorry for Freddie having to lug it about everywhere, but Freddie said he didn't mind. He felt it was making him stronger and I had to admit, he seemed to be getting fitter by the day.

'Can you imagine playing at Goodison Park?' I said, pulling on my coat. 'This is a proper ground where the men play. The girls are so excited. Lily said she could barely sleep.'

I couldn't help feeling a bit jealous myself. What must it be like to be good enough to play football in front of so many fans?

'Well, I don't envy you,' Mam said. 'It's a bitter-cold day all right. You need to wrap up warm. I don't want the lot of you catching your death. That's all I need.'

'We'll wrap up,' Hettie said. 'I only wish you'd come, Mam. You might like it if only you were to watch a game?'

'Oh, why would I want to watch a daft game of football? I'm happy to stay behind and have some peace and quiet.' Her eyes grazed the front door. 'Besides, I want to be here. Just in case I'm needed, like.'

Hettie nodded. She didn't have to say any more. We all knew she was worried about Dad. She would want to be here, waiting for him in case she was needed.

Once again, I was forced to push the nagging feelings about Dad to the back of my mind.

Not today, Martha. Not today.

Today I want to be happy.

And happy I was on the bus travelling to Goodison Park. I was so lucky that Hettie had got Freddie and I seats on the rickety bone-shaker. Immediately, I was swept up in the atmosphere on board as we travelled to Liverpool. Some of the girls, like Lily, were quiet and sitting deep in their thoughts. I wondered if they were a bit nervous, or simply just collecting themselves before the big game. Other girls, like Alice, were louder and more chatty – lighting up the journey with laughter and bursts of song, one of which they had made up themselves:

When upon the fields of play we go: thousands come and cheer us on our way
And you will often hear them say: Who can beat Dick, Kerr's today?
When the ball is swinging merrily, faces beaming happily
So play up girls and do your best, for victory is our cry.

What you couldn't see or hear, though, was the energy that seemed to buzz between each girl. It was difficult to describe, but it was there all right – a force that seemed to burn brightly in each and every one of them. It was almost as if they were connected in some way.

Hettie was sat beside me. She was quite quiet, too, and halfway through the journey she squeezed my hand.

'I'm nervous for them, you know?' she whispered.

'I am too.'

'All this build up. There will be so many eyes on us and the St Helen's girls. I really want this to be a great game. I want the critics to be put wrong. I want them to see that women's football is just as good as the men's game.'

I gently squeezed her hand in return. 'They will see, Hettie. How can they not?'

She shook her head. 'There are some daft folk out there, I just don't understand it . . .'

We were quiet for a little longer and then carefully, I spoke up again. 'Hettie? Does it make you sad that you're not still part of it . . . you know, not part of the team; properly playing?'

I could see she was chewing on the inside of her cheek, thinking this over. 'Well, yes. Of course, I'd love to play with the girls, Martha. It would be a dream, it really would. But my knee will never be strong enough and, if I'm honest, I'd never be as good as the first team players now. They are head and shoulders above where I was.' She turned to face me. 'Why are you asking?'

'I don't know really . . . I suppose I wonder sometimes – what will happen if I don't make it into the team.'

'Why do you think that?'

I shrugged. 'I'm not very fast, Hettie, and if I'm honest, I do struggle at training. I still love playing football, but I can see I'm not as good as the others.'

'But you can get better. With training,' she said. 'You're still so young.'

I thought of Lily and the other young players who were already so much better than me and smiled sadly. 'Maybe.'

'And if not, there may be other things you can do,' Hettie said. 'It broke my heart when I stopped playing, but look at me now.' She spread out her arms, indicating to the team. 'I'm still part of the Dick, Kerr Girls. They are still my sisters. There are still ways you can belong.'

I nodded, my thoughts rippling within me.

That was it, totally. I just wanted to be a proper part of this.

I wanted to find my place in the Dick, Kerr story.

It was beyond amazing inside the Goodison ground. I stood, squeezed in next to Freddie, pitchside, because there simply wasn't enough room available in the stands. Freddie reckoned there were many thousands more fans than the thirty thousand Hettie had predicted. Not quite double, but close! I could feel their weight and excitement weighing down on me. The chanting and singing lit up the entire ground; everywhere I looked I could see bodies, shiny faces and fluttering scarves. When we had arrived, the crowds had been overwhelming and a police escort had been waiting to take the team in safely. I had watched as the girls moved quickly off the bus, their faces pale with shock. It was all a little bit too much to believe. In fact, it was quite extraordinary.

Hettie hurried over to us. She had been chatting to the girls and Mr Frankland before kick-off – she always liked to wish them well.

'Mr Frankland says there are more people outside the ground.' She breathed hard; her cheeks flushed red. 'There are at least ten thousand out there that can't get inside, but they are standing there anyway. They all want to be here!'

'And people still say there's no place for women's football.' Freddie grinned, preparing his camera. 'I want to get some pictures of this crowd. The lads won't believe it back in the office.'

'Imagine if they were all to get inside of here,' I said. 'It'd be more than any men's game, wouldn't it?'

'Except these people are coming to watch our factory girls from Lancashire,' Hettie said, smiling. 'Imagine that. That's how important our girls have become.'

I stood back, trying to take in the sight. It really was unbelievable. The noise was quite deafening, and as the teams ran on to the pitch the crowds' cheers exploded even more. I couldn't begin to imagine how our girls were feeling. I watched as Alice ran to each of her team, patting them on the back and having a quiet word. I imagined she was doing her best to calm everyone's nerves and if anyone could do it, it was Alice Kell. My eyes grazed the team. I quickly realised there was someone missing.

'Where is Flo?' I asked, my voice rising.

Hettie sighed. 'She's not here, Marth. She's been in Paris and was having to catch a train to meet us here. I'm guessing her train was late or she missed the connection. Mr Frankland is upset, but we will have to start without her. Jennie Harris is playing up front today.'

I frowned. That really was a bitter blow. Flo was our most prolific goalscorer. We needed her more than ever today. What a shame that she would miss such an important match as this.

I wasn't even on the pitch and my stomach was already doing loop de loops.

I gripped Freddie's arm. 'I hope they'll be all right, with all this pressure and without Flo.'

Freddie still had his face pressed up to the camera, his aim directed at the gathering teams. 'Aye. This is the Dick, Kerr Girls we are talking about, lass. Pressure is what they deal with best.' He removed the camera and turned to face me. 'They will play well for Flo. They'll do it for her.'

The game was kicked off in style by music-hall star Ella Retford. As she sang 'She's a Lassie from Lancashire', I could feel my tummy begin to settle. Especially as the crowd joined in. It was impossible not to feel happy.

The first half passed in a blur of activity. Both teams were fast and furious and looking to impress, but it was the Dick, Kerr Girls that scored first. Lily Lee passed the ball up through the centre and Jennie Harris picked it up neatly at the outside of the box. Jennie might've been one of the smallest players on the pitch, but she was also one of the most powerful. Her driven shot slotted into the back of the net with no resistance.

For the second half, Mr Frankland decided to move the players around a bit and put Alice Kell in centre-forward position.

'That's unusual,' I remarked. 'Alice usually plays in defence.'

Hettie grinned. 'You wait and see. Alice can be great upfront.'

Hettie was right; Alice seemed to come alive in her new position – perhaps fired up by the thought of her missing friend – and she quickly scored her first goal, a clever volley outside of the box. This was followed by a shot into the top corner and a neat tap in from a corner kick.

'A hat-trick!' Hettie said, jumping up and down on the spot. 'She will be pleased.'

By the final whistle, the Dick, Kerr Girls were 4–0 up and in total command of the game. All the fans in the crowd seemed to be chanting their name.

We stood and watched as the Lord Mayor of Liverpool presented the team with a silver cup. Each girl also received a medal as a gift of thanks from the ex-servicemen's families for all the money they had helped raise for charity. I could see the tears shimmering in the girls' eyes. This meant so much to them.

'They must have raised a few thousand today,' Hettie told us. 'It's amazing, it really is.'

'They are amazing. The crowd, the money raised,' I said softly. 'Nothing can stop them now.'

I didn't realise how wrong I could be.

The first weeks of January passed by and at first, everything seemed to be going so well. I managed to go back to school with a slight spring in my step. I was still caught in the memories of that wonderful Boxing Day game. I could even ignore the scolding from Mrs Penny as she told me off time and time again for daydreaming, by imagining that one day I might be a player on a pitch like Goodison Park. My knuckles became quite sore from being rapped by her heavy ruler!

But it didn't matter. I had such hope that better things were coming.

Training was still proving to be tricky, even though I tried my absolute best. The girls were so kind, too – they never teased me for lagging behind or for not having the strength that they all did, but at times it was hard not to let the frustration bite at me.

'I only wish I could keep up,' I muttered to Lily one time, as I was bent double after a race. I was still trying to catch my breath and my sides felt like they could split open with pain. Lily had run back to check that I was all right. She often did this, or shouted encouragement to keep me going. She liked to help me where she could. She was good at that.

'You shouldn't be so hard on yourself,' Lily had replied gently. 'You will get better with more practice.'

I had nodded, only hoping that she was right. It was hard to ignore the doubt that was still niggling me, though. I could see how far ahead the others were. Especially Lily. I would often stand back and simply watch her, completely in awe of her talent. She seemed to be able to control the ball with no effort at all, almost as if it were tied to her feet. For Lily, football was as natural as breathing was to anyone else. As soon as the football was at her feet, Lily's face would light up, her eyes would sparkle and her body would roar into action.

I knew that I needed to keep practising, but finding the time was proving hard. Mam was needing my help more and more around the house and it wasn't like I could play with the lads outside now.

'You needn't worry so much, Martha. Just try and enjoy yourself,' Lily said.

'I know, but . . .' I pushed back a strand of sweaty hair. 'I worry that I'm not good enough. What else am I good at, really?'

I thought of school. I thought of how much I hated the lessons. I wasn't good at needlework or cooking. Where did I fit in? Football was my only love.

'You'll find your place.' She chuckled softly. 'We're still so young, Martha. You have the whole world in front of you. We both do.'

'Aye – you do, that's for sure.'

'And you do too. Don't forget that.' Lily's voice was firm now. 'You need to believe in yourself more.' Her gaze skirted over the other girls, who had gathered together at the other side of the field. 'We'd better catch them up, or we'll end up missing the next exercise. Do you feel up to it?'

I nodded. 'Yes. Of course.'

Her hand gently squeezed mine. 'Come on, then.'

I shivered slightly at her touch.

'I wish I was like you,' I told her. 'You were born for all of this.'

Lily simply smiled shyly. 'Ah, you daft beggar. I'm nowt special.'

But I noticed the smile remained on her face as we

jogged back to meet the other girls. I could see how important this all was to her.

And I realised too, with a slight tug in my stomach, how important she was becoming to me.

I came home to voices in the living room. I immediately recognised the deep and solemn tone of Mrs Taylor from down the road. My blood chilled in my body immediately. If she was here, it couldn't be good news. Rather than go in, I stood just outside the open door. I knew this was a bad thing to do and Mam would scold me if she saw me loitering like this, but I also knew that it was the only way I was likely to find out what was happening. Everyone still treated me like the baby of the family. Silly, daft Martha who shouldn't be bothered with burdens or problems, but I knew I deserved to know the truth.

'. . . you need to listen to Mrs Taylor, love . . .' My mam's voice. I could hear the wobble in it. Had she been crying?

'I will not!' My dad's. Louder now, but with a crack in it, like he was straining himself. 'This is nonsense. Ruddy nonsense. I can't stop work like that. I can't.'

'I'm not a doctor . . .' Mrs Taylor now. She was

calm but firm. '. . . but I can see how poorly you are. You're sweating, and your breathing isn't right at all. I think you need to rest. Perhaps you should consider calling out a doctor now?'

'Doctor!' Dad huffed. 'We can't afford doctors, who do you think we are? I'll not have any of those toffee-nosed people round here.'

'Hospital, then,' she said quietly. 'Just to check you over.'

'You should be in a hospital,' Mam said quietly. 'You know you should go, love.'

'No.' Dad's voice, louder now. 'I don't want to be in one of those places. I told you before. Besides, they'll still expect payment. We can't afford it.'

'It'll be supplemented,' Mrs Taylor said gently. 'You won't have to pay the full amount.'

'Oh yes . . . because some rich beggar felt sorry for us poor paupers.' Dad coughed. 'I don't take charity; I pay my own way.'

'But with Freddie and Hettie earning . . .' Mam insisted. 'We could afford a night? Maybe two?'

'And you forget I've already been docked for having time off.' I heard movement in the room. 'I won't have it. I'll keep working all the time I can, while I still have breath in my body. I don't want our hard-earned money wasted.'

'But don't you think he should go?' Mam's voice was pleading now. 'Tell him, Mrs Taylor, that you think he should.'

'I can't tell him anything of the sort.' Mrs Taylor huffed. Then I heard her sigh. Her voice softened. 'But I do think the docks will be the worst place for you. If you're not in hospital, you should be here, with your family. You should be . . .'

I couldn't listen to it any more. With tears stinging my eyes, I left the house silently and slipped back into the street.

Outside, the lads were playing. I sat quietly on the wall as they knocked the ball about, their shouts ringing out into the air. It wasn't so long ago that I would've been out there with them, not a care in the world. I saw Davey look over. His eyes fixed on mine, and he smiled shyly. For a second, I was tempted to run over. To forget about the argument we'd had before, and just play again. I could pretend that my life was back to how it used to be.

I could be back to running rings around the lads at football.

I wouldn't be fretting about Dad, or my future.

Everything would be all right again.

I didn't like this new Martha. She was too heavy. Too full of worries. It was making everything so difficult.

I kicked my legs against the wall. Then, slowly, I got up and walked away.

I couldn't join the lads. Not today. Not ever.

Everything had changed now.

Later that night, I curled up beside Hettie in the bed. Usually, we slept apart from one another, too hot and flustered to get too close, but tonight I needed her near to me. Hettie had got home late from the factory, tired and glum. However, I'd heard her talking quietly to Mam in the kitchen while I was practising in the yard. I knew they had been talking about Dad. Once again, their voices dropped as I'd walked into the room.

Freddie wasn't even here. He was away covering a match down in London. I missed his gentle snores from the other bed. I longed to sit with him and be comforted by his words. Freddie always knew the right things to say. He always knew how to make me feel better.

'I know Dad is sick,' I whispered. 'Really sick.'

Hettie took my hand and gently squeezed it but didn't say a word.

'How bad is he, Hettie?'

She sighed. 'I don't know, pet.'

'He looks . . . different, doesn't he? Thinner. And his skin . . .' I shuddered. 'I don't like it.'

'There's no point upsetting yourself, Marth. There's nowt you can do.' Her voice was so quiet, I could barely hear it. 'You know Dad. You know how he is. But he's strong, too. Stronger than we think.'

But was he? Really? Dad had faced so many battles. His accident years ago had weakened his body and although he never spoke about it, we all knew he spent his days racked with pain. Surely there was only so much a man could take?

'Try not to worry,' Hettie said. 'Things can change.'

'I just think . . .' I hesitated, not wanting to let the words go. 'I just think he's really bad this time. What if . . .'

My voice cracked. I swallowed hard. I felt my body shiver. Hettie squeezed my hand again.

'We don't focus on what ifs,' she said. 'That's no good for anyone. You need to get some sleep and turn your brain off for a little while. Things will look better in the morning. They always do.'

I nodded, my eyes glistening with tears as I continued to lie pressed up against my sister, my hand still tightly gripped in her own cool hand. I listened as her breathing became regular and soft, and her grip slowly released mine.

Then I carefully peeled myself away, turned on my back and stared up at the dark ceiling. The morning seemed a long way away and for once, I was not looking forward to it coming. I really wasn't sure that Hettie was right.

How could things look better in the morning?

How could things ever look better again?

It was the training sessions that kept me going. I also loved spending time with Lily. Simply being with her lifted my spirits and I wasn't even sure I could explain why. I suppose there was something about her calm and kind attitude that I liked and, even better, she was funny; she could make all the girls curl up with her daft jokes. She was so clever and wise, and she could also tell if I was struggling. She didn't ask too many questions, she could clearly see that made me more upset, but she became like a protective cloud next to me – making sure I was all right, reassuring me when I made yet another mistake in training, and causing me to laugh when my spirits took another beating. She and the team always knew how to make things better.

I suppose Hettie was right, too – there was something about being with the Dick, Kerr Girls that made everything feel good. I could forget about school, or my worries about Dad, and simply enjoy the time with the team. It didn't even matter that I wasn't a proper member, not really. They always made me feel included.

I knew Hettie was worried, though. The past few days she had been acting strange and mardy. I thought at first that she was worried about Dad, like me. Only yesterday, she had been stomping around the bedroom like an angry elephant. But, it turned out, all those meddling people had been complaining about women's football again and Mr Frankland had heard that this time, they were going all the way to the Football Association. Freddie had heard the same, at work, and said as much. I don't think that helped to improve Hettie's mood.

I tried not to worry too much about Hettie's concerns at training. After all, the team had faced similar complaints before. Surely, it would all blow over.

It had to, didn't it?

Because if not, what then? What would become of the Dick, Kerr Girls?

Today's training ended and as usual, I found myself exhausted and a little bit disappointed with my own performance. However, I tried not to be too hard on myself.

I found myself glancing over at Lily as she was taking off her boots and getting ready to ride home. Her mam was coming to see her today and by all accounts they were very close. Lily was full of excited chatter. I wondered if she had heard the rumours that Hettie had spoken of. I wasn't sure whether to mention it or not. I certainly didn't want to worry her if she hadn't. What would be the point in that? I'd hate to be the one to make Lily Parr sad.

'I can't wait to tell my mam about the games coming up,' Lily said, her cheeks glowing with pride. 'Mam says I could be the best forward in the country. She really believes in me.'

I forced a grin back, my gaze fixed on Lily's face. 'That's grand, Lil.'

She really was so pretty. Her eyes sparkled when she was excited, and her smile was so warm and sweet. It was hard not to be drawn to her. How could I tell her what might be happening to women's football? It would break her heart.

I couldn't stand for that to happen. I think that would break mine in two as well . . .

'Ey up! Why are you staring at me like that, you daft beggar?' She laughed, flapping her hand in front of my face. 'Have I suddenly sprouted two noses?'

I giggled, my cheeks burning red. 'N-no . . .' I stuttered. 'I was just lost in thought.'

Luckily for me, Lily rushed off without paying much more heed, keen to get back to meet her mam. I watched as she slung her bag over her shoulder and balanced herself carefully on her bike. She waved to all of us.

'See you at the game, girls!'

We watched as she rode away, the wind whipping through her hair as she moved down the road, as graceful and agile as a whippet.

'Aye, our Lily is a good lass,' I heard Alice Norris say behind me. 'As strong as an ox, and fast, too. I think she has been the making of us.'

A few of the girls murmured their approval. I could see Alice was still smiling with approval. It was clear how protective and fond of Lily that Alice was and that the two girls were very close. I couldn't help feeling a stab of jealousy in the pit of my stomach.

'She's certainly the talk of Preston,' Flo said brightly, gathering her belongings together. 'I heard some lads talking the other day. They were admiring her, saying she was good wife material.'

Alice Norris burst out laughing. 'Don't tell our Lil that, I don't think she'd like to be seen as good wife material by anyone.'

Jessie giggled. 'It's true, though – she's getting a lot of attention. I think many lads are in awe of her. And nice ones too. I bet she would have her pick of them, should she want to, of course . . .'

'Lucky Lil,' Flo declared, and the rest of the girls roared with laughter.

'She's only fifteen,' Alice Kell said firmly. 'I'd wager the lass has no time for silly lads, and good for her.'

I stood back shyly, pretending to be taking off my boots, but I was watching Alice Norris carefully. I could see the tiny frown on her face. I saw how her head was shaking a little.

'Most of the lads that follow me about are gormless,' Flo was complaining. 'Maybe I need to have Lil on my arm. Perhaps she attracts a better class of fella.'

'That's true,' Jessie agreed. 'What type of lad does Lil like, Alice? Does she even say? She's so quiet about that sort of thing, you'd never be able to guess.'

'I bet she likes them big and strong,' Flo said.

Alice Norris's cheeks were pink now. She continued to shake her head. 'Err . . . well, I don't know. I'm not sure they're really her type. If you get what I mean . . .'

Flo looked up, her eyes bright with interest. 'No . . . I don't know what you mean. What are you saying?'

I kept myself busy with my laces, but really I was keen to hear more of the conversation. Anything related to Lily grabbed my interest.

Alice began to hurriedly pack her kit away. 'I shouldn't be gossiping. This is Lil's business. If you have any questions, you should be asking her, not me.'

'Aw, Ali, don't get all serious. We're only messing.'

Alice Kell stepped forward and laid a protective hand on Alice Norris's shoulder. 'Let's leave this now, eh? I can see Ali is getting upset.'

Flo shrugged, but I could tell she was a little taken aback. 'We didn't mean any harm, Alice. I just wanted to know a bit more about my teammate. There's no harm in that, is there? I wouldn't like to put my foot in it with her or anything.'

'No. Of course not, but I don't want anyone getting upset,' Alice Kell replied.

Alice Norris picked up her bag. She faced Flo

and smiled weakly. 'I'm not upset, really I'm not. I just don't like chatting about Lil behind her back. It's not a big thing. But I know she's quite private about her life. She would worry that people might think badly of her.'

'Why would we do that?' Jessie asked softly. 'We love our Lil.'

Alice sighed. 'If I tell you, do you swear not to tell another soul?' Her gaze swept across all of us. 'I'm only telling you, so that you don't keep pestering her about lads, or asking her awkward questions or asking her awkward questions – she'd hate all that. It might be better for her if you know.'

'Only if you're sure,' Alice Kell said sternly. 'But we won't breathe a word, I promise. I can vouch for all the girls here.'

Alice Norris nodded, like she had finally made up her mind. 'All right, well, it's quite simple really. Our Lil doesn't like lads – not in that way anyway. She never has. She likes girls.'

Flo's eyes widened. 'You mean, romantically?'

'Yes, romantically.'

'Oh . . .' Flo said slowly. 'I mean . . . that's all right, isn't it? It makes no difference to us.'

'She's happy,' Alice said. 'But she doesn't like to talk about it, all right? So, I don't want you lot pestering her.'

'We won't,' Alice Kell said. 'You have our word.'

Alice Norris seemed to sag with relief. 'Well . . . that's all right then.'

'It's really not that a big a deal,' Jessie muttered, slinging her bag on to her arm. 'It just means more lads for the rest of us.'

Alice Norris grinned. 'I knew you would all understand. I will tell Lily I told you. It'll be nice for her to know that you won't treat her any differently.'

'Why would we?' Alice Kell asked. 'Nothing's changed, has it?'

Everyone nodded with agreement, murmuring their approval, including me. My mind was swirling with the information. I'd never known of a girl liking other girls in that way before. Was it common? Was I just a foolish child for not knowing these things?

Alice Norris turned and noticed me lurking. 'Oh! Are you all right, lass? I didn't see you there. You look lost in thought.'

I smiled back. 'Oh, I'm fine.'

I stood and picked up my bag, ready to leave.

There had been a lot to take in, but one fact still remained firmly planted in my mind. Lily was important to me. In fact, she was becoming the best friend I'd ever had.

Nothing had to change, did it?

However, later that night, everything did change. For me, anyway.

Hettie was full of chatter about a boy she had started talking to at the Dick, Kerr factory – Jimmy Flowers. Oh, just to hear her, you could tell she was full of excitement.

'He's going to take me to the pictures, Marth. He's a proper gent. He's speaks all lovely, too.'

Even though we were tucked up in bed in the dark, I knew her cheeks were flushing as she spoke; she kept giggling as she described his good looks to me. How he was tall, blonde and strong.

'How does he make you feel?' I whispered.

'Oh . . . so tingly. Like someone is touching my skin, all over,' she breathed. 'And he makes my stomach flutter every time I talk to him. In fact, I can't stop looking at him. I feel so warm and alive every time I do.'

'That sounds wonderful . . .'

'You probably think I'm daft.' She turned in bed, took my hands in hers. 'But one day, a boy will make you feel this way. You will be full of joy, like a thousand bubbles are jiggling in your tummy.'

'Maybe . . .' I whispered back.

I watched as Hettie fell into a light sleep, her thoughts obviously still fixed on her beloved Jimmy. I couldn't rest. My brain was whirring and my eyes remained fixed open.

How could I tell Hettie that I was already feeling all of these things that she described?

Was it possible that I could feel them for another girl?

Was I falling for Lily Parr?

10

As January slipped into February, Hettie came home one day a little more excited than usual.

'You look chirpy,' Mam said, her eyes glinting. She had been hovering in the kitchen, waiting for Dad to come home. Despite her insistence, he was still going off to work every day – telling her to 'stop mithering'. It did mean that every evening she lingered by the front door, eagerly waiting his arrival. I knew it was such a relief to her when he came home in one piece.

'We had some good news today,' Hettie said, tugging off her coat. 'Do you remember that Harry Weldon is doing the pantomime in Liverpool?'

Harry Weldon was a comedian that I knew Mam quite liked.

Mam clapped her hands to her chest. 'Aye, I do. He's so funny. Mrs Daniels saw him a few months back and said that she fell off her chair laughing.'

'He's grand,' Hettie said, nodding. 'And he's come

up with an idea to organise a charity fancy-dress carnival alongside a football match. All the money raised will go to unemployed ex-service men, the Liverpool Hospital and the children's fund. Isn't that good? He's even donating a cup as the prize.'

'I'm guessing that will be named after him,' Freddie said.

'Well, yes. I suppose so. But it will be grand to win it.'

'Sounds a great day,' I agreed. 'I take it the Dick, Kerr Girls will be playing?'

'Of course.' Hettie grinned. 'This will be a great opportunity for them. It might put those doubters to bed. They will be playing a team made up of the best players from the rest of the UK – not just England this time! It was all Harry's idea. He thought it might be a good-humoured attempt to 'put one over' on the invincible Dick, Kerr Girls. He's lining it up to be played at Anfield of all places!'

'Put one over our girls?' I snorted. 'I don't think that will happen, do you?'

'Will it heck as like,' Hettie said. 'But it puts us right back in the public eye, doesn't it? They have to see how important we are.'

'Or how dangerous,' Mam said quietly.

We both stared at her and she blinked back at us, like she had surprised herself with her words.

'I'm just saying, that's all . . .' she said. 'You make yourself look too good, the best in the whole country, and it might make more people want you gone.'

Hettie shook her head. 'That's not the case, Mam.'

But I saw a worried expression drift into Hettie's eyes. I knew she was rattled.

The day of the carnival was upon us in no time. I was so excited, not least because I had been invited to take part in the procession with the rest of the team through the streets of Liverpool. I was a little surprised at this, but Mr Frankland had insisted on it, laying a gentle hand on my shoulder.

'You could be a future player for the team, lass. You have every right to walk alongside them.'

I still felt a little odd marching beside the other girls, worried that I looked out of place. Pride still burnt within me though. I couldn't quite believe I was amongst this group, wearing their kit and smiling brightly out to the crowds. It was all so strange and wonderful at the same time.

Lily was just up ahead, walking beside Alice Norris. Lily was smiling shyly at the crowds, who were shouting her name the loudest. I felt a glow of pride watching her. How humble she was. She was often in the newspapers these days, and only recently the *Stalybridge Reporter* had been full of praise after her performance in the St Helen's game. Freddie had brought the piece home to show us – it had been so favourable to many of the girls, but Lily Parr had stood out to them the most. I had read the article over and over, my skin tingling at the mention of her name. It made me so happy that others could see how special she was, like I did. I had read it so many times I could recite it back, parrot-fashion. The *Reporter* called her the 'new kid on the block' and then went on to say:

Taking sex into consideration there is probably no greater football prodigy in the whole country than Miss Parr. Not only does she have speed and excellent ball control, but her admirable physique enables her to brush off opposing defenders. She amazes the crowd wherever she goes by the way she crosses the ball clean across the goalmouth to the waiting forward.

As we continued to walk, I felt like the crowd around me was fading away. All I could see was Lily, moving in front of me. The stomp of my feet on the hard surface was like the beating of my own heart, fluttering fast in my chest. In fact, it was beating so fast, I feared it might burst clear from me.

Lily. Beautiful. Strong. Lily.

She turned suddenly, as if she could feel my eyes upon her. Her gentle gaze held mine.

And then, Lily being Lily, she pulled a daft face to try and make me laugh. She always did that. She always liked to make me smile.

That was just how sweet Lily was.

She cared about me.

And that feeling alone lit a bonfire inside my heart.

Anfield felt full and lively. I stood on the sidelines, still wearing the Dick, Kerr kit even though I wouldn't be asked to play. I stared around the ground in awe. How did the girls get used to playing in front of such huge crowds? It was beyond me. I heard mutterings that there were over twenty-five thousand people here to watch them. That number seemed so huge, so unbelievable, and yet, I wasn't surprised.

So many people wanted to see our team play. The huge group of photographers and newsreel cameras gathered on the pitch also proved how popular they were. The team would be plastered all over the papers and apparently would be appearing on Pathé News, so people might also get to see them on the newsreels at the cinema!

I caught sight of Freddie jostling for position to get the best shot. He was getting stronger and stronger. I happily watched as he broke free to the front and snapped a photo of the girls as they ran out. He always managed to get a good one.

The doubters were idiots, I thought to myself. They needed to come and watch for themselves. If they only did that, then their daft objections might go away.

I shook my head sadly. Why wasn't anything ever that simple?

The game passed in a blur. I was lost in thought for most of it, but I was lifted by the Dick, Kerr Girls' amazingly strong performance. They quickly showed who was the best team, even if they were playing against some of the finest footballers from around the country. Hettie had told me one player had travelled from as far as the Shetland Isles. That would seem an even longer journey home after a defeat.

The Dick, Kerr Girls were soon 3–0 up, thanks to goals by Lily. I watched, mesmerised, as she tore through the defence on each occasion and thundered the ball into the back of the net. It really was as if she was on fire. In the game, she was strong, fierce and frightening. The opposition didn't quite know what to do with her! The Rest of the UK team managed to claw one goal back in the first half, but it was the second half when things really came alive.

I watched, open-mouthed, as Lily scored two more extraordinary goals, taking her tally to five. Flo, obviously keen to get in on the action, picked up two of her own, as did Jennie Harris. The opposition looked battered and exhausted.

The final score was 9–1.

The girls swarmed Lily, patting her on the back and pulling her into a hug. She looked sheepish and awkward again, almost as if she couldn't quite believe what she had just done.

I remembered the reporter's article.

There is probably no greater football prodigy in the whole country than Miss Parr.

I don't think there had ever been a truer word said.

I came home to find Dad sitting in the kitchen. He must've come home early from work because it was unusual to see him home before six.

'Where's Mam?' I asked.

'Ah, she's popped over to see Mrs Taylor, lass. That woman will not stop going on about me. I keep telling her I'm all right. I just need to sit quietly for a bit.'

Dad didn't look all right, though. I could see by the way he was hunched over that he was struggling for breath. His skin had a sweaty sheen to it and his hands, which were laid out on the table in front of him, were shaking slightly.

'I had to knock off early,' he said, like he knew the questions that were bubbling inside of me. 'The foreman said it was clear I could barely lift a thing. He told me to take the week off, get my strength back.' He shook his head. 'The other lads are beginning to talk. They make excuses for me. I'll not have that . . .'

'But Dad, if you need to rest . . .'

His steely gaze met mine. 'If I can't work, lass, what have I got? What use am I to you all then?'

I slid into the seat opposite him. Gently, I laid my hand on top of his. My skin was so white compared to his. He felt so rough and cold. He had big hands, my dad. Big, strong hands. Hands that could lift things, mend things, make things better.

'Do you remember when I was little and you made me that doll's house out of the old crate you found at work?'

Dad hesitated for a moment and then a smile settled on his face. 'Oh, aye, I do. I spent ages on that thing, banging it into shape. You'd been asking for one, but we couldn't afford a posh one from the shop. It weren't anything grand . . .'

'It was perfect.' I squeezed his hand. 'It was the best present I ever had. It was the best because you made it.'

Dad shook his head. 'I can't do anything like that now. I get so tired. So damn tired . . .'

'It must be horrible for you, Dad. But it doesn't matter to us that you can't do these things any more. It just matters to us that you are still here, with us.' I could feel the tears biting in my eyes. 'All the rest of it, it doesn't matter really – not now. Hettie and Freddie help out. I'll be earning soon.'

He smacked his lips together. 'You're just a little girl, Martha.'

'I finish school in a year or so, Dad, and I want a job. I want to work in a factory like lots of the other girls round here do. I think I'd be good at it.'

'But why? You don't need to now. The war is over. You don't need to do your bit. You can find a nice husband . . .'

Husband? My skin grew cold at the thought. I pulled my hand away from Dad. What would he think if he could see inside my mind? If he knew that Lily Parr was the only person I wanted. How I dreamt of touching her. Kissing her . . .

My body trembling, I turned away from him.

'I don't want a husband, Dad. Things are different now. I want to work and earn my own money. I want to help Mam; help the household.'

There was a brief silence, and then finally Dad nodded. 'Aye, of course you do. Out of the three of you, you are my brightest spark. I know you will do well, whatever choice you make, lass. I don't pretend to understand this world we live in now, but I'm learning to accept. I can see you have a place in it. I'm so proud of you.'

I smiled sheepishly.

'I just wish your mother would hurry up,' he muttered.

'She loves you so much,' I said. 'She just wants you to get better. She wants to do everything she can.'

'Aye, and I love her too.' Dad was looking straight at me again, his eyes fixed on mine. It was like he could see right into me. 'One day, you will have it too, Martha. You will find someone you love so much you will do anything for them. It will burn your heart and it will tear at your soul, but there will be no other feeling like it.'

'Maybe . . .' I whispered.

'Maybe?' He chuckled. 'A lovely lass like you? There's no doubt about it. Love will hit you when you least expect it but, by gum, you'll know it when it happens.'

I smiled shyly back. 'Thanks, Dad.'

But all I wanted to do was grab his hand back in mine and tell him the truth. In fact, shout it from the rooftops.

'Dad . . . I know this feeling. I'm feeling it already.'

'Dad, can you help me? I feel so sick. So unsteady. It's driving me mad.'

And, more importantly, 'Dad, what do I do? I've fallen in love with a girl. Will you accept that? Will you still hold my hand tightly in yours? Will you still say you're proud of me?'

But of course, none of those words flowed from me. Instead, we sat in silence, waiting for Mam to return.

11

The weeks after the Anfield game seemed to rush past in a frenzy, and soon we were hurtling into the warmer months of spring. I was beginning to wonder where the time had actually gone; it was getting hard to find time to even catch my breath.

School continued to be as dull and painful as it had always been. Now that my mind was settled on factory work, I found it even more difficult to sit still inside the drafty classroom. My thoughts were constantly drifting elsewhere.

'Martha. Head up. Pay attention!' Mrs Penny barked at me more than once. 'You won't get anywhere with your head in the clouds, you know?'

I just stared back at her, muttering my apologies. All I knew was, I wouldn't get anywhere in this daft, boring school.

My distracted mood wasn't helped by the fact that I was seeing less and less of Lily, which was such a shame. We had been on one more brief bike ride, the weekend after the Anfield game, but since then, the Dick, Kerr Girls had been busy playing matches. Most recently, they had been up in Scotland raising more funds for charity. The scorelines had been incredible: 9–0 at Celtic Park and 13–0 at Edinburgh. The team really were carving out a reputation now. As a result, Hettie's mood had improved.

'With results like this, the nay-sayers will be ignored, won't they,' she said. 'No one in their right mind would stop our girls now.'

'I doubt it,' Freddie said, but I noticed his tone was quieter. I wondered if he'd heard differently at the newspaper. I meant to ask him, but he was so often out of the house it was difficult to find a moment to talk.

In fact, a lot of the time I found myself on my own, practising with my ball, lost in my own thoughts and memories.

On our last trip out, Lily had been quite calm about it all. As we sat on the blanket, in a field by the side of the esplanade of Miller Park, she had seemed quite unbothered about all the recent criticisms.

'We're just footballers,' she said, munching her sandwich. 'Very good footballers. If you took our sex out of this, there would be no fuss or bother. Everyone would be simply remarking on our speed and skills and would stop harking on about the fact that we wear bloomers under our shorts.'

I giggled. 'You're right, Lil. It's so daft.' I considered it for a moment. 'They should be comparing you to the greatest footballers around.'

'Oh, don't be daft.' Lily flapped her hand at me. 'I'm no better than the rest of the team.'

'You're too modest.'

'Am I heck as like.'

We both chuckled, but we knew she was. Lily didn't like the attention on her. She knew she was a good player, but she didn't want fuss or bother made about it and she didn't like the spotlight being drawn away from the rest of the team. I think that's what I loved about her. She could shine so brightly, but she wouldn't let her shine diminish others. I thought it was a very special and unique thing.

Lily laid back so that she was resting on her elbows. She tipped her face up towards the sky. I stared at the tilt of her elegant chin, at the curl of her lips as they broke into a smile.

'Ey up! I can see a face in the clouds. Look!'

I shifted closer to her and then gently eased myself down so that I was lying beside her. We were so close our arms were touching. I could feel my skin prickle. My stomach was turning over and over like the waves in the sea. I felt sure she would notice, but Lily was still staring up into the sky. She reached up and pointed.

'Look! Look at that cloud. I swear it looks like Mr Frankland.'

I turned my attention to the sky, squinting up at the swirling white balls of fluff.

'I can't see anything . . .'

Lily rolled towards me, on to her side. I could feel her warm breath on my neck.

'Look . . .' she said softly, pointing again. 'Look there, towards the left. That large white cloud. Can you see the longish nose? The chin . . .'

I stared again. The clouds seemed to be shifting and moving into place. It was like a picture was slowly being revealed.

'By gum, yes! It is Mr Frankland! Even the shape of his head!'

Lily was still so close to me. She giggled softly. 'You just have to look. Then you can see it.'

I hesitated. Right there, right in that moment, I longed to tell her. I wanted to turn so that I was facing her, so that our faces were inches apart. I could touch her hair. I could look deep into her eyes. I could say it.

'Lily, all I can see is you right now . . .'

I felt the words form inside of me. The confidence was beginning to build. I forced back the lump inside my throat.

'Lily . . .'

'Aye?'

'I-I . . .' I stuttered. What would she say? Would she laugh? Would she no longer want to be my friend? I would hate that more than anything.

I swallowed, tasting dry air.

'What is it?' she asked, nudging me. 'Cat got your tongue.'

'I . . . I was just thinking. That cloud there looks like my teacher. It even has her moustache.'

Lily roared with laughter, rolling over on to her back. It was almost a relief to have her move away. I wasn't sure my nerves could take much more.

'You are a daft apeth, Martha,' she said, shaking her head. 'You make me chuckle.'

'Do I?'

'Of course you do. You're my pal,' she said. 'I'm so glad to have met you.'

'I'm glad too,' I replied.

But, as I thought back on those words that were said, I regretted not saying more.

I regretted being such a coward.

I was still regretting it now.

Dad was sitting outside, watching the lads playing football in the street as I came back from school. His expression seemed wistful and lost in thought. I watched him for a moment or two before approaching. He sat back, as if startled by my presence.

'Ey up, lass, you're back early.'

'There's no training while the girls are away, so I came straight back after school.' I joined him on the low wall. I nodded briefly at the lads, who seemed to be having more of a scrap than a football game. 'Enjoying it?'

He chuckled. 'It's all right, I suppose. You should join them, Martha. You'd probably be able to show them a thing or two.'

I stared over at the gang. One of the other lads from

the street, Will Mercer, now had the ball and was making a clumsy run over the cobbles. I remembered the late evenings when I used to join them. How the hours used to fly by while I tackled and raced past them. It all seemed so long ago now.

Dad lay one of his meaty hands gently on my knee.

'You can talk to them, lass. Ask them to let you play again. Pride only gets you so far, you know.'

'They don't want me, Dad. They told me as much.'

'Ah. Lads say things they don't mean. We all do. You need to pay no mind to that.' He drew out a long breath. 'Life is too short to bear grudges. If you want to play, go and play.'

I straightened my shoulders, my eyes drifting again to the game in front of me. It was so tempting to just slip off the wall and run over there. To slap the lads on the back and pretend that nothing had happened between us. After all, Alfie wasn't around. He couldn't ruin my fun. But something was holding me back. A heavy, claw-like feeling was pinning me to that wall.

'I'll just sit here, Dad, if that's all right,' I said. 'I think that's all I want to do.'

'Aye, all right. If you're sure?' he replied gently.

I nodded. I was sure. I no longer belonged with the lads on the street. I was no longer the same girl that used to run around with them, without a care in the world.

Everything was changing for me.

Later that month, I travelled down with Hettie to watch the Dick, Kerr Girls play the French Ladies again. It was quite an exciting event, after the team had toured France last year. Of course, the French players were keen to try and beat us again, even though they were a lovely bunch. Hettie wanted me to meet them for myself. The game was being played in Staffordshire, so we went along with the team in their rickety coach.

Once again, everyone was in high spirits and the usual songs and laughter lit up the journey. This time, however, I had the pleasure of sitting next to Lily, which of course made everything even brighter.

'Are you excited?' I asked her.

Lily nodded keenly. 'It was great fun playing these girls before. They're a right strong team. I just hope I play well.'

I nudged her gently. 'Lily! Of course you will. What would stop you?'

She shrugged. 'It does no good being too sure of yourself. I just want to enjoy the game.' She rubbed at her stomach. 'I'm a bit nervous, that's for sure. Do you have any food in your bag? It might settle my jitters.'

I giggled. This was so typical of Lily. I swear if she wasn't a footballer, she'd make a great chef.

'I've only got a humbug,' I said, digging it out of my bag. 'You can suck on that.'

Lily plucked it from my fingers. 'Perfect.'

I watched as she plopped into her mouth, swirling it around like it was the greatest gift ever.

'You, Marth, are my saviour.'

'And don't I know it!'

'Are we still going for a bike ride this weekend?'

'Oh, aye.' I smiled. 'You try and stop me.'

'Bring more of these humbugs,' she said, her words muffled by the huge sweet. 'They're really good.'

The game itself was wonderful. I stood with the other fifteen thousand spectators, my body pressed up against the stand, keen to take in every piece of action. I still hoped that one day I would be good enough to join the girls on the pitch, but, watching them play – seeing how strong and fast they all were – I knew I still had a long way to go.

'I'll keep trying, though,' I muttered to myself. 'I won't give up.'

'Eh? What was that?'

Hettie was stood next to me. I felt myself blush, wishing I hadn't been caught talking to myself.

'I just said, Lily doesn't stop trying. She won't give up.'

'Oh, that's one way of putting it.' Hettie laughed. 'It's like there's three of her out there now.'

I knew what she meant – Lily was playing the game of her life. Every time I thought I had seen her play her best, Lily would come out and perform even better.

She had quickly scored the first two goals and then, after half-time, had managed to drive in two more, putting the girls 4–1 ahead. Throughout the game, she was commanding the attack and controlling the pace. She looked unbeatable.

'I don't think she can do much more,' I said.

'Are you sure about that?' Hettie said, pointing. For, just as I'd spoken, Lily was back inside the penalty box. The ball was lofted in by Alice Kell and Lily met it sweetly with her head, drilling it into the top corner.

5–1. All five goals were Lily's.

'That girl is one of the best things that ever happened to our team,' Hettie breathed.

'Yes,' I whispered. 'She really is.'

12

You could tell it was July – the air was thick with summer haze and the sky was completely blue. Unlike our previous bike trip, there wasn't a cloud to be seen.

Lily was chattier than usual as we rode leisurely up the hill towards the park. I was happy to listen, finding that I didn't have much to say. Once again, I was distracted with worries about my dad. He hadn't gone to work today. He was lying in bed when I left and Mam had told me not to disturb him as he hadn't slept well. I ended up lingering by the door instead, imagining him behind it. I hoped that he was resting and would wake feeling much better.

We stopped in our usual place and Lily laid out her blanket. Lily was full of excited chatter about the boxer Georges Carpentier meeting them all before their recent match. It was one I had missed because I had been helping Mam at home, but Freddie had told us all about it. According to Freddie, Georges was one the best boxers in Europe and the fact that he was lending his support to the Dick, Kerr Girls had sent positive waves through the sporting community.

'He was very decent,' Lily said. 'Very polite, not what you would imagine at all. And he said the funniest thing to me.'

'What was that?' I asked.

'He said he wouldn't want to face me on the pitch.' She laughed. 'He reckoned I would be too fast and fierce even for the likes of him. Can you imagine? He's a great hulking lump of muscle and he wouldn't want to play against me!'

'Well, to be fair, I'd say you'd beat him on the pitch,' I said. 'He wouldn't have your skills, Lil.'

Lily pulled a face. 'No – he was just being nice, that's all. He spoke to all the girls. Flo was a blubbering mess, of course. He wasn't even much to look at.'

I laughed. 'You weren't impressed, then?'

'He's not my type. Barely a hair on his head, and far too old.' She screwed up her nose. 'I can't see the attraction, to be honest.'

'So . . .' My finger trailed the loose thread on the rug. Did I dare ask? The words were leaping about in my head, fighting to be asked. 'So . . . what is your type, Lil?'

She held my gaze for a second. It was steady and unwavering, her expression deadly serious, and then slowly, she pulled away. She began rooting around her bag, clearly looking for a distraction.

'Aw, Marth, I'm not sure really,' she muttered. 'I'm a fussy old thing.'

'But—'

'Look!' She pulled out a wrapped slice of cake. 'I bought this earlier today. Let's have a bit, eh? I'm starving. And then we can talk about you for a change. I'm sick to death of nattering about me. It's so dull.'

'It's really not,' I said.

She unwrapped the cake. 'Oh, trust me, lass. It is. I can't think of anything I hate more.'

I wiped the crumbs from my lap and reached for the bottle of pop at the edge of the rug. Lily was stretched out next to me, her expression lost in thought once again. She seemed so relaxed and peaceful. Quite unlike the footballer she was on the pitch. It was almost as if there were two Lily Parrs. The confident, skilful forward with high energy, strength and determination and the quieter, shyer girl who was happy to sit quietly and listen to the sounds around her. I really did love both versions of her; they both fascinated me.

'So . . .' she said finally. 'We were going to talk about you . . .'

'If we have to.' I smiled. 'I'm not sure there's very much to say.'

'Of course there is. Don't put yourself down so much.' She sat up. 'How is school? Are you still hating it?'

'Oh, yes.' I sighed. 'I can't wait for it to be over. I think Mrs Penny is sick of the sight of me.'

'And then what? What will you do when school is finished?'

'I've asked Hettie to ask Mr Frankland about some work at the factory. He knows what a hard worker I am, so I'm hoping . . .' I shrugged. 'It's more difficult now. There are more men looking for jobs, so less need for girls like me.'

Lily nodded. 'There's still work though, if you look hard enough. So many men are still injured or struggling after the war, and we lost so many, too . . .' Her voice drifted. 'Women are doing well in the workplace too. I really think times are changing, Martha. Soon it won't be so unusual for women to be doing men's work – and not just in times of war.'

'You think?'

'I do think. There's no reason now to hold us back. People can see that we are just as good. More managers like Mr Frankland will see that too.'

'And maybe those that oppose it will change their minds...'

'I dunno.' Lily frowned. 'There will always be folk that are set in their ways. I know many will never be happy to see women playing a man's game.'

'That makes me sad,' I muttered. 'And scared they will try to stop it.'

'We just have to hope that they won't,' she replied. 'We have to do everything we can to rise above it.'

'I guess...'

She gently patted my arm. 'Try not to worry. There's nowt you can do about other folk, you just have to concentrate on your own journey. Yours and no one else's.' She paused. 'Are you still finding the training difficult?'

'Sometimes. I'm still not as fast as the rest of you. I struggle to keep up and my skills aren't as polished.'

'You'll get there, lass.'

'Maybe...'

'Are you coming on the Isle of Wight trip?' she asked.

I sighed. 'I can't. I don't want to leave Mam at the

moment; things are tricky at home . . .' I hesitated, not really sure I wanted to tell her more just yet. 'And I'm not up to scratch, Lily. I'm not ready to travel with the team. I need to improve first.'

'Don't be so hard on yourself.'

'It's true though. I'm so far behind.'

'It's practice, that's all. Are you doing any training at home?'

'I was, but . . .'

My throat tightened. I shook my head.

'I-I'm finding it hard to think about other things,' I stuttered. 'Things are difficult right now . . .'

Lily squeezed my arm. 'Martha? Are you all right? You look so pale.'

'I-I just . . .'

But it was too late. The tears were flowing.

I soon found that I was swept up in Lily Parr's arms, crying noisily on her shoulder, feeling suddenly like my entire heart was about to shatter into pieces.

'It's my dad,' I explained finally, swiping at my damp nose. 'He's so ill. I've never seen him look this poorly. He can't even go to work.'

'Oh, Martha,' Lily said gently. 'You poor thing. You must be so worried.'

'I am. I'm trying so hard not to be, but it's all I can think of.' I paused, trying to compose myself, but it was hard when my nose was running and my eyes were gushing tears. I must've looked such a mess. I turned my face away from Lily, suddenly ashamed. 'They are all so used to me being the happy one. That's me – Martha, who makes everyone laugh. I don't usually fret like Hettie and Freddie do, but this time it's too hard not to. I can't keep pretending everything is all right. It feels wrong to do so.'

'I understand that,' Lily said. 'I think I would be just the same.'

'I try and go out in the yard, knock the ball around like I used to, but it's difficult to focus – my mind keeps trailing off. Usually I'd practise with Freddie, but he's working longer and longer hours. I reckon he finds it too hard being at home. I know he worries, too.'

'You shouldn't worry about the training, lass. It'll come when you're ready.'

'Maybe . . .' I shook my head. 'I'll never make the team playing like I am at the moment though.'

'There's no rush, is there?' Lily's voice was calm. 'It sounds to me like you have bigger things to think about right now. You can only put your mind to one thing at time or you'll give yourself a right old headache.'

I smiled despite myself and wiped my nose again. 'But look at you, you're only a bit older than me and you're already so much better . . .'

'Ah, don't look at me.' Lily sniffed. 'I'm nowt special, really. I just work hard, that's all, and I have nothing else to bother me. I'm lucky to be doing something I love. I can focus all of my attention on it, can't I. I'm sure if I had things going on elsewhere it would affect me too.'

I blinked and smiled weakly at her. I was grateful for her kind words, but we both knew Lily was special. She was head and shoulders above everyone else. I'd wager if she had the entire world's problems on her shoulders, she would still play a wonderful game.

I wasn't Lily Parr.

'You should play with other people. Some younger lads maybe?' she suggested. 'It could help your confidence.'

'The lads in my street don't like me playing with them any more. They think I show off. They say that I've got ideas above my station.'

Lily burst into a fit of giggles. 'Oh, they do, do they?

Well, that's even more reason to play with them. To prove that you are no such thing. You're not going to let a group of daft lads stop you, are you?'

'I guess not.'

'I'm telling you now. I'll never let a daft lad stop *me*. Or some jumped-up critic,' she said, louder now. 'They can complain all they like, write their silly little letters into the newspaper, but I won't stop playing, not for anyone. This is what I do. It's all I know.'

We sat for a while in comfortable silence. I rolled up my tissue and stuffed it up my sleeve. I took a sip of drink and sat back to enjoy the view. My thoughts were still sad, still full of worries about Dad, but it was like a small weight had been lifted. I felt lighter – almost as if I could float up and drift into the clouds themselves.

'You look miles away,' Lily said finally. 'What are you thinking about?'

'That it would be wonderful to fly.'

Lily grinned. 'Martha, you are a daft lass. You make me chuckle. Where did that come from?'

I tipped my head back. 'I'm just imagining what it would be like to be free. To float across the sky. It must feel wonderful.'

'I dare say . . .' Lily didn't sound sure. 'Although, I think I prefer my feet firmly planted on the floor.'

I laughed. Lily always had a way of making me feel better.

'It'll be all right, you know, in the end,' she said. 'Things work out as they're meant to. I really believe that.'

'I hope you're right.'

'I do, too.'

'I'm going to miss you, Lil,' I said without thinking. Immediately, I felt my stomach twist. Why did I say that? Lily would think me so needy, so childish. It wasn't even like she would be gone for that long.

But it was true, I would miss her. I always did when she was away. I would've loved to have gone on the Isle of Wight trip and, to be fair, maybe I could've if I'd demanded it, but I knew I could never leave Mam with Dad so poorly. Hettie would already be going and Freddie too, to take the photographs. One of us had to stay behind.

'I'll soon be back,' Lily said brightly. 'We can arrange another bike trip. I'll tell you all the news. I'm sure there will be plenty.'

I nodded. 'I'd like that.'

She moved closer towards me; our heads were almost touching. I could feel her breath against my ear. 'I'm your friend, Martha, always. If you've got a problem, you can come and find me, all right? If I can help. I will.'

I turned my face slightly. We were so close. I'd never really looked at her eyes this closely before. Brown and warm like bright conkers. It was all I could do not to reach up and touch her cheek. She was so pretty.

'Lily . . .'

'What? What is it?'

'I . . .'

Oh. Why couldn't I say it? Why couldn't I tell her how I felt?

Instead, I bowed my head again. The spell was broken. My doubts swept back over me like a wave.

'We had better go . . .' I muttered. 'It's getting late. I need to check on Dad.'

'No problem.' Lily sprung up on her heels. 'But not before we've finished this cake. Everything feels better when you've had a bit of sugar.'

I nodded meekly, but somehow I wasn't so sure.

13

As the Dick, Kerr Girls left for their Isle of Wight trip, I couldn't help feeling sad still. I longed to be on the coach with them all. I imagined how excited they all would be. Instead, I waved goodbye to Freddie and Hettie and forced my disappointment to the back of my mind. I didn't want them to notice – it would only make them feel bad too. There was no sense in that.

Hettie pulled me into a tight hug. 'It's only a few days,' she said. 'Will you be all right?'

'Of course I will,' I said, forcing a grin. 'I've got enough on my plate here. Mam will have me run ragged.'

'Oh, I'm sure she will.' I saw Hettie's gaze linger at the living room door. 'Will you keep an eye on Dad too? I know that Mam is looking after him well, but you cheer him up. He needs that.'

'You think I cheer him up?' I asked.

Hettie grinned and lightly planted a kiss on the top of my head. 'It's what you do best, lass.'

After they left, I slipped into the living room and pulled up a chair next to Dad's bed. He often slept well into the morning now. Mam had to sleep on the floor beside him to give him more room. She said he wasn't sleeping at night at all now. He had to have pillows propped up behind his back or else he found it difficult to breathe. Mam said it was that which kept him awake the most – the fact that he couldn't catch his breath. It sounded horrible, like he was slowly drowning.

Outside, I could hear the lads playing. There was the familiar thud of the football hitting the cobbles. I felt a tug inside of me. How I longed to join them. What would they say if I did?

Dad was awake. He smiled weakly as I sat down.

'Hettie and Fred have gone, then?'

'Aye. They were going to say goodbye, but they didn't want to disturb you in case you were sleeping.'

He rubbed his eyes. 'I don't do much of that, to be honest. Never mind, they'll be back before we know it. How exciting, eh? These girls don't half get around. France, the Isle of Wight . . .' He coughed into his hand. 'They've seen more of the world then I have.'

'Hettie reckons there will be more besides,' I said.

'Mr Frankland has plans to take them all over the world. Their reputation is growing. There's even talk that America want to them come.'

'America?' Dad breathed out. 'By 'eck, that's impressive for sure.'

'It really is.'

'Maybe one day you'll be with them, lass. There's no reason why not . . .'

'Oh . . . I'm not so sure about that.'

Dad wriggled on the bed, adjusting the pillows behind him. 'I'm getting out of this thing today. Your mam may go on about me resting, but I feel like I'm wasting away here. I need air.' His eyes glinted as he looked at me. 'We can go outside. You can show me these skills of yours.'

'Dad, I'm not sure . . .' I picked at the cover on his bed. 'I can show you. But I don't want you to be disappointed.'

He scoffed. 'Disappointed? Why would I be? I used to watch you out there playing with the lads. Back then, I questioned why any lass would want to play such a rough game, but I was daft in the brain in those days . . .' He shook his head slowly. 'But even then, even when I doubted it, I could still see you were a bit special. You would leave those boys on their backsides.'

I giggled, despite myself. 'You used to tell me off. You'd tell me to go and do something more useful.'

'Yeah, well, I knew no better then.' He sighed. 'I'm an old man, Martha. I'm stuck in my ways, but the funny thing is . . . when you get to the end of your life – you, well . . . you start to appreciate things more. Things you took for granted before.'

'The end?' My skin grew cold. 'Dad . . . don't say that . . .'

'There's nothing to fear, lass. Nothing,' he said firmly. 'And I think it's about time you realised that for yourself. I'm resigned to my fate, and you need to be, too.' He began to heave himself up. 'I don't intend to sit around here feeling sorry for myself and I don't want you to, either. So, are you going to take me outside, or what?'

The same lads were outside. It made me sad to see them. Only a few months before I would've run over to join them, but now I hung back. I could see Alfie was there, and he was the last person I wanted to face. A makeshift football pitch had been arranged just to the right of our house. Dad eased himself into his usual position on the low wall and waved casually in their direction.

'You see. You should go and join them.'

I hesitated. 'I'm not sure they'll want that.'

'And what? You're suddenly scared now?' He sniffed. 'I didn't think that was you, Martha. I thought you faced up to people and didn't take any nonsense. This is your street as well. You have every right to play if you want to.'

I thought of Lily, of what she had said to me before. I could almost feel her giving me a hard shove between the shoulder blades.

'All right, all right . . . I'll go.'

Alfie looked up as I approached. He had the ball and kicked it over towards Davey.

'Oh, look what the cat's brought in,' he sneered. 'You come to show us how to play?'

'No . . . no, not at all.' I scuffed at the ground with my feet. 'I just want to play, that's all.' I looked over at Ronnie. 'C'mon, Ron, we used to have fun.'

Ronnie scowled. 'Yeah, we used to, until you started getting all bossy.'

'I didn't though – that's not fair and you know it,' I said, feeling my anger rise. 'I just want us to play properly and to the rules. If I was another lad, someone like Alfie, you wouldn't get so mardy about it. This is only because I'm a girl, isn't it!'

I saw Ronnie's cheeks redden. 'It's not that at all . . .' he started, but before he could say anything more, Alfie came over, clearly rattled that I'd mentioned his name.

'Oh, aye – the best footballer in the town is back. Tell us, Martha, have you actually played a game for the Dick, Kerr Girls yet? Because last I heard, you were sat on your backside just watching them.'

The fire in my belly was burning more furiously. I tried to keep my voice level and not show Alfie just how upset I was. I knew Dad was watching all of this. I didn't want him to get angry and come over. That wouldn't be good for him.

'I'm watching them, yes. But I'm still part of the team. I train with them. I'm getting stronger and better.' I looked Alfie up and down, taking in his reedy, weak body. A thin smile settled on my lips. 'Which is more than I can say for some . . .'

Despite themselves, Davey and Ronnie chuckled. This warmed me a little. I realised I wasn't on such a weak footing. These two lads used to be my friends, after all. And what was Alfie, really? Just a loudmouth who thought he knew it all. A bully. Dad had always told me what to do about bullies – you didn't let them see that they were getting to you. You rose above them.

I straightened my shoulders; suddenly I felt ten feet taller.

'You only don't want me to play because you know I'm twenty times better than you. You're scared, that's all,' I said. 'Scared of a girl.'

Alfie snorted. He glanced at the rest of the boys, who were now gathered around behind him, looking fascinated by the whole scene. 'Get her,' he said loudly. 'She actually thinks she's better than us.'

I glanced over at Dad, knowing he would have been alerted by Alfie's raised voice. He was now standing up and looking like he was about to approach. I made a face at him and gently gestured with my hand that he should sit back down. I was all right. I could deal with this on my own. It was about time.

'I never said I was better than you lot,' I said carefully, my eyes drilling into Alfie. 'Only you, Alfie. And you hate that. It's what winds you up.'

'I'm not worried about you,' he sneered.

'Then show me. We can each take a turn on goal, see how many shots we get past Davey out of ten. I bet I'll score more than you.'

I saw Alfie's face twitch a little. He was stuck and he knew it. Everyone knew he was usually poor at taking shots – most of the time he scuffed the ball or hit it with the wrong part of his foot. The only thing Alfie was good at was pushing other lads around and bulldozing his way through the game. Alfie had a problem now. If he took on my challenge, he was likely to lose and look daft in front of everyone, but if he refused, he would look weak and cowardly and show himself up.

'So, what will it be?' I said, placing my hands on my hips. 'I ain't got all day.'

Alfie looked around him and then back at me. 'I ain't got to prove myself to anyone, least of all you.'

'You haven't answered the question.'

He snorted again and then kicked away the ball that was just in front of him. 'You daft lads can do what you like, but I'm not standing around to hear this lass squawking at me. I've got better things to do.'

'I'm sure you have.'

'I'm going to the green,' he said, turning to the others. 'Who's coming with me?'

Davey hesitated. 'We're in the middle of a game here, Alfie.'

'Yeah, and we've gotta go in soon. There's no sense in going too far,' Ronnie added.

Alfie's scowl deepened. 'You lot are wet. You stay here and play with this girl if you want. You're turning soft like rest of them, just like my dad said. All the idiots that think women should be doing everything we do are making it worse for us. It won't be long before there's nowt left for us men.'

'That's daft, Alfie, and you know it,' I said. 'There's more than enough for everyone.'

His eyes were gleaming now. 'You reckon, do you? Well, there's plenty that say different. My dad says there's those that are fighting to stop this nonsense. They know that it's a bad thing to take away the things that men do. It's not right. It's not normal.'

The word 'normal' stung me like a bee sting. I flinched. Alfie noticed and grinned.

'Go on – go and have your game now. You may as well, it won't last.' He flapped a hand in my dad's direction. 'Even your dad will be pleased when things go back to normal – because they will, Martha. My dad has heard talk. He knows important people. The Dick, Kerr Girls will soon be stopped. You mark my words. So have your fun while you still can.'

And with that, he stalked off, whistling under his breath like he really didn't care.

'Pay no mind to him, Martha,' Davey said kindly. 'He gets all worked up, but I'm sure he knows nothing.'

'Yeah, come and join us, take Alfie's place,' Ronnie said. 'We've missed you, you know. Even the bossing.' He chuckled shyly. 'Well, maybe not so much that.'

'I'm not bossy,' I said. 'I'm just trying to help you, that's all.'

Ronnie kicked the ball towards me, and I received it gratefully. It was good to be back again; back with my friends, back doing what I loved doing most.

But Alfie's words sat heavy in my heart.

I only hoped that he was wrong.

Dad took my arm as we walked back into the house.

'It was good to see you out there again,' he said. 'Having fun, showing the lads what you can do.'

'It was good, Dad.'

He squeezed me gently. 'I like seeing you happy,

Martha. I really do. I hope it'll always be the case for you. That's all I want for all three of you, really. Happiness. It's such an important thing.'

'I know . . .'

'I might not have been the best dad, but remember what I said, all right? Tell the others too. I only want the best for you all.'

'Dad . . . I . . .' I didn't like this conversation, it was making me feel upset.

'C'mon, you daft thing, let's get you into the house before your mam has both our guts for garters. Our dinner will be cold.'

I smiled weakly at him, knowing I couldn't find the right words to say.

Knowing that we were both fighting back the tears.

By the end of August, I could feel my mood lifting. Some aspects of my life had improved – I was enjoying playing outside with the lads again and pleased that Alfie no longer seemed to be putting in an appearance. I'm not sure if it was his hurt pride that kept him away, but the other lads quietly admitted that they were pleased to see the back of him. It seemed I wasn't the only one that hated his bullying tactics, but I had been the only one to stand up to them. That was something I was very proud of. Practising with the lads also seemed to help my confidence and as I returned to training with the Dick, Kerr Girls, I didn't feel so desperately behind. Alice even took me to one side and said she was noticing how strong and fast I was becoming. This made me glow with hope.

Hettie kept herself busy at the factory and Freddie was forever at the newspaper or out at games taking photographs. I think we were all dealing with our worries by keeping busy. It was a shock, then, the day Hettie came home from the work in a foul mood – fouler than I'd ever seen before.

She stormed into the kitchen, where Freddie and I had been chatting quietly whilst Mam was cooking. She sat down hard on the chair and sighed loudly.

'Hettie!' Mam said. 'You needn't crash into the house like that. You nearly took the front door off its hinges. Remember your poor dad is trying to rest.'

Hettie's face paled. 'Sorry, Mam, I wasn't thinking. I came home in such a rush. I . . .'

She trailed off, shaking her head. Freddie reached across and patted her hand.

'Are you all right, our kid? You look done in.'

'It really has been quite a day,' she muttered. 'I've been talking to Mr Frankland for hours. We're both so angry. I've got a headache from all of it. You won't believe what is happening.'

'What is it? What's happening?' I asked.

She sighed, then spread out her hands and attempted to explain. Her voice was still shaking. 'There's rumours – we don't know where from or how they started, but these rumours suggest that the money in ladies' football teams isn't being managed properly.'

'But that's nonsense, surely?' Freddie asked. 'Who is saying this?'

'I don't know who, but we all know plenty of folk want women's football to stop. There is too much support for it, and we are raising so much money for charity, perhaps some people are getting jealous and want to cause trouble for us. I don't know . . .'

'But are teams managing the money inappropriately? That's a wild accusation,' Freddie said. 'Is there any evidence of that?'

'I don't think so,' Hettie said. 'The money we raise goes directly to the charities. I mean, there have been huge amounts raised, which might make some folk suspicious. But there's been no reason to suspect any wrongdoing. All women's teams we know act in total accordance with the rules.'

'So, what happens now?' I asked. 'Surely these silly accusations will come to nothing?'

Hettie frowned. 'I don't think so. The Football Association are going to take more control of our games. They want stricter control of our finances, and they want to be involved more heavily in the running of things.'

'But that's not so bad, is it? If we haven't got anything to hide?' I asked hopefully.

Hettie shook her head. 'You don't understand, Martha, this is just the start. Mr Frankland thinks the Football Association are just finding anything they can to destroy us. After all, there is no basis to these claims – none at all! They are picking holes and making accusations that don't exist. This has been the plan all long. To find something to discredit women's football with.'

'But . . . but what will this mean?'

'It means that the FA might have found their reason to stop us playing altogether.' Hettie's eyes shone with tears. 'This really could be the beginning of the end.'

I was due to meet Lily the next afternoon for another bike ride, but she didn't feel up to riding very far. So instead, we decided to go for a short walk to the green. I could tell Lily was cross. Her face was pinched and pale. It was clear that the word had reached the factory about the Football Association and all the Dick, Kerr Girls had been rocked by the news.

'Mr Frankland was telling Alice,' Lily explained.

'He was so upset and of course, as our captain, Alice had to tell the rest of us. She's up in arms over it all and not sure what to do.'

'It might still be a fuss over nothing, Lil,' I said, trying desperately to reassure her. I hated seeing her so unhappy. 'Perhaps they will look closer at how the clubs are run and see that there's no problem and then they will leave us alone. Surely they don't want the bother?'

Lily snorted. 'Sometimes, lass, you can be so naive. This isn't about money or anything like that. This is about a group of men, sitting high up in football offices, who are trying to find a way to make it difficult for women's football to flourish.'

'I still don't understand why they would, though.' I saw Lily's frown and tried desperately to explain myself. 'I know there are plenty of people that are against us playing, there has been since we first started. But for every single person that hates women playing football, there's another ten or so that love it. Surely the Football Association can see that? Look at the crowds that come to our games! The money we raise! The newspapers love us . . .' I shook my head. 'It makes no sense to me.'

'We are the biggest club in the country and it still doesn't matter,' Lily replied quietly. 'We are women. Simple girls. And them blokes in power don't like that. I'd wager that they don't like the attention being taken away from the men's teams. We are becoming too popular for our own good – and it worries them.'

'There's room for both.'

'You'd think so, wouldn't you?' Lily sighed. 'It's all so daft, Martha. I am sick of fighting it. We are footballers, and good ones at that. It shouldn't matter what sex we are, or what is or isn't dangling between our legs. Surely it's only the game that matters?'

We had stopped walking and were standing under a large oak tree. Lily was quite visibly shaken, and turned away from me slightly. I wondered if she was about to cry. I wasn't sure that Lily would want me to see that.

Gently, I touched her arm and Lily turned to face me.

'Lil – it will be all right,' I said, making my voice sound more confident than I felt inside. I needed Lily to believe me. 'You and the girls are so good at what you do, nothing will stop that. You wait and see.'

'I can't stop playing football, Martha,' she whispered, her eyes blinking at me. 'It's what I do best. It's when I feel at my most happy. How can I stop?'

'You won't, Lily. You won't have to. It won't come to that.'

'But these people . . .' She flapped her hand in rage. 'They don't see it like us. They just think we are a nuisance. Something to stop at all costs.'

'So then – we fight back.' I squeezed her arm tightly, trying to make her see. 'We fight, Lily. Like we always have. Like the suffragettes have done for us. We'll take our turn.'

'Martha . . .' Lily stared right into my eyes; a tingle snaked down my spine. It was all I could do not to look away. Her expression was so warm, so loving. Was this it? Was she about to tell me she loved me? I shivered.

This was the right time. Surely?

'Lily . . . I . . .'

'What is it? Martha . . .' Her voice so gentle now.

'Lil . . . I think . . . Well, I know . . . that I really like you . . .'

'Martha—'

'I like you . . .' I swallowed, the words were so

hard to say, but I had to say them. I just had to. I felt I would burst otherwise. 'I mean, I really, really like you. Not just as a friend ... I can't stop thinking about you. I—'

'No.' Lily stepped back, her eyes wide. 'Don't say it ...'

I felt my body stiffen with embarrassment. Had I got this so wrong?

'I thought you'd be happy ...' I stuttered.

'No, Martha. I'm sorry. I didn't mean for this to happen.'

I blinked, tears building. 'What do you mean? I thought you felt the same? You are so kind to me, so loving ...'

'Because you are like a sister to me.' Lily shook her head. 'I'm sorry, Martha. I couldn't see you in any other way.'

'I-I ...'

I was shaking. My cheeks aflame. How could I have been so daft? I wished I could suck the words I had just said back into my mouth. I wished I could run and hide for ever.

I had ruined everything.

Lily touched my shoulder.

'Martha, please. Let's talk about this. We need to.'

'No . . . I need to go. I need to . . .'

My thoughts were jumbled, my words not even making sense now. I couldn't stand to look at Lily. I couldn't bear to see whatever expression would be showing in her eyes. Was she disgusted with me? Disappointed? Or, even worse, did she pity me?

I turned to leave.

'MARTHA!'

Another voice, not Lily's. I turned instinctively towards the sound. At first I couldn't see anything, but then, suddenly I could. It was Freddie, hurrying towards us. His cheeks were bright red and his hair ruffled, as if he'd been running for ages. I stepped away from Lily, aware of how close we were still standing. She felt a million miles from me now.

'Martha!' He ran towards us. 'I've been looking all over. Mam said you'd gone for a walk, but it was so hard to find you.'

'What is it? Whatever is the matter?' I stared at Freddie, blinking. A bad feeling washed over me. All the shame and disappointment had disappeared and now there was only a coldness settling into my bones. I felt stiff and unyielding, barely able to move.

'M-Martha . . .' he stuttered. 'I'm sorry. I'm sorry to disturb you, but you need to come home.'

'What is it, Fred? What's happened?'

I knew the answer before he'd even said the words. His sorrowful eyes told me everything. My legs were suddenly jelly. I wished I hadn't asked.

I didn't want to know.

'It's Dad . . .' he said quietly. 'He collapsed.'

15

I ran all the way home. I don't think I've ever moved as quick. Freddie and I didn't speak – we didn't need to. The unsaid words were floating between us like heavy bubbles. Was this it? Would Dad be all right? Would we make it back in time?

Was this my punishment for not being with him? For wasting my time with a girl who didn't feel the same way about me?

I rubbed at my eyes, trying to push back the tears.

Yes, it was. This was all my fault.

This was my payback.

I should have been with Dad, not Lily.

I should have put him first.

As we ran into the street, Freddie took my hand.

'Are you all right, our kid?'

'I think so,' I said, although my heart was thumping like a hammer in my chest. I wasn't sure I was ready to admit to Freddie just how scared I actually was. 'Is Hettie home?'

Freddie shook his head. 'I'm not sure where she is. I went to see Alice and she said she's gone to some meeting with Mr Frankland, that it was something to do with the team and that FA decision. Alice is going to try and find out where she is.'

'She needs to be here,' I said. 'Mam is going to be so worried, being there on her own.'

'The doctor will be there too. Mam was going to fetch him.'

'Dad always says we can't afford a doctor,' I replied, shocked.

'Well, we'll find the money somehow. Me and Hettie will help,' Freddie replied. 'If I could, I'd take him to hospital. That's where he should be, but Dad won't agree to it. He's says he won't take handouts from rich folk.'

Bitterness swirled inside of me. I could understand why proud men like my father didn't want to have to rely on charity to pay for his hospital care when he was sick. Dad worked just as hard as, if not harder than, any fella born with a silver spoon in his mouth.

The world just felt so desperately unfair.

I blinked back the tears; it was all I could do not to yell into the sky.

Freddie squeezed my hand again. 'It'll be all right, our kid,' he whispered. 'Try not to fret.'

But his words sounded hollow and broken.

Dad was in his bed again. The curtains were tightly drawn. He appeared to be asleep, but I sat myself down next to him anyway, keen to be there when his eyes opened. It was such a relief to see his chest rise and fall – it instantly made my own breathing calm.

In the next room, I could hear Mam murmuring and the unfamiliar sound of a man's voice. I assumed it must be the doctor. I raised an eyebrow at Freddie.

'I'll go in there and see what's what,' Freddie said. 'You stay with Dad. Keep him company.'

I nodded. I had little intention of doing anything else.

The living room, which was such a familiar sight to me, now suddenly felt different. It was smaller somehow, and darker. There was a heavy smell in the air, of sweat and something else that I didn't recognise. I stared at the man on the bed – my dad. He was sunken back into the pillow, his hair plastered against his face as if it was wet. His lips were lined with a ghostly grey mark and his cheeks looked hollow and aged.

'Oh, Dad . . .' I breathed.

'Martha . . .'

His eyes opened slowly, painfully. He turned his head ever so slightly to face me.

'Martha, is that you?'

'Yes, yes, Dad, it is. I came home as soon as I heard.' I touched his blanket and tried to keep my voice calm. 'Freddie said you had become unwell.'

He licked his lips. 'Yes . . . I . . . I don't know what happened . . . I . . .'

'Dad. You don't need to speak. It's all right, really. Just rest for now.'

'She . . . your mam got the doctor in. I told her not to.'

'Mam was worried, Dad. You're not well.'

'We can't afford . . .'

His voice drifted and his eyes closed again. I reached under the blanket and found his hand. It felt cold and heavy in mine. I rubbed it gently, attempted to warm it up, to do anything that might be of use.

'You mustn't worry . . .' he whispered, his eyes still shut.

'Dad. Hush now. You need to sleep.'

'You . . . you need to prepare, Martha. All of you . . .'

'Dad. Please. You don't need to be talking.' I was panicking now. 'You need to rest up.'

He took another desperate breath.

'. . . you need to prepare for life without me.'

Later, I sat in the kitchen with Mam. Hettie had come home and had rushed in to see Dad. Now both she and Freddie were with him. We were taking turns. I think we were all scared that something would happen if we were to turn our backs.

Mam looked exhausted. She insisted on making us both a cup of tea, before sitting herself in front of me. I looked at the dark rings around her eyes and wondered if she had been sleeping at all.

'What did the doctor say?' I asked.

'It was his heart, he thinks. It's failing,' Mam said quietly. 'He needs to rest, to sleep, but there's not much else that can be done.'

'Not much else? I don't understand.'

'Martha, it's his heart. Once that gives up, that's it.' She blinked, wiping her mouth. 'I knew he was poorly. He's been getting weaker and weaker. His breathing and everything . . .'

'So, what do we do?'

'I don't know. We wait, I suppose,' Mam replied. 'We just wait and see what happens.'

'But that's awful. That's like we are giving up on him!'

Mam stared at me; her eyes were shining. 'I'm not giving up on him, Martha. I'll never give up on him. But I'm not a miracle worker. There's only so much I can do.' Her body sank back into the chair. 'I wish I could do more. I really do, but I can't.'

Everything was different in the house after that. We each moved like ghosts from room to room, barely speaking and simply existing. Mam insisted that Freddie and Hettie still had to go to work. We needed their money, after all. Mam wasn't sure if she would need to call the doctor in again, but it would be costly if she did. I still went to school but was finding it even more difficult to concentrate. Once the final bell rang, I'd run home, ignoring the cries from the lads on the street outside. I no longer wanted to play with them. I no longer wanted to train or even think about football. It all seemed so pointless now.

My place was at home.

We did what we could. Mam made Dad food that was easy to eat. She washed his face. She sat and talked to him long into the night, sleeping on the floor beside him so that he could rest in their bed.

We continued to take turns sitting with him. Sometimes I would read to him, other times I'd simply watch him sleep. He was doing a lot of that lately. Mam said he was like a newborn baby again – needing care and rest.

Except he wasn't like a baby at all. Babies grew older. Babies stopped being needy.

With every passing day, Dad just seemed to be slipping further and further away from us.

I'd missed a few training sessions, but Mam insisted I went to the next. Even though I felt tired and fed up after school, she said I needed fresh air and exercise. She told me I should put my mind to other things.

I didn't want to go but I agreed, to please her. After all, she had enough to worry about. But the thought of seeing Lily again made my body squirm. How could I face her now? I felt so silly after saying what I had. For what I had told her, as my Dad had been struggling for breath. In the end, I simply had to hope she would stay away from me. That would be best for both of us. Easiest.

As soon as I arrived, I could tell there was a heavy mood hanging over the girls. I listened to the chatter amongst them as I began putting my boots on, and it was clear that the threat of the Football Association's restrictions was still causing concern. I could see that Lily was engrossed in a deep conversation with Alice Norris, Alice Kell and Flo. I was glad, as it gave me an excuse to stay away – although I did notice that Lily flashed me a shy smile. I think she was surprised to see me there. I turned away. I really wasn't sure what else to do.

The training session itself was a disaster. It was clear that none of us were in the right frame of mind, and we were all struggling to concentrate. Our coach had to shout to bring our attention back to focus. Even Lily wasn't looking as sharp as usual.

But it was me that was struggling the most.

My head was so cloudy, and my entire body felt heavy and leaden, almost like it didn't want to perform. I found that my attention was drifting off and our coach was shouting at me the most, to try and snap me back into line.

It wasn't working. My thoughts kept returning to Dad. Was he asleep or awake? Was he all right? What if he had taken a turn for the worse?

Shouldn't I be there with him, just in case?

It felt so wrong simply being here.

By the time the final practice game came, I felt exhausted and drained. I had been placed in defence, a position I wasn't best suited to. Usually, I'd give it a go and try my best, but today, all I wanted to do was sink to my knees and give up. I suppose that's why I failed to notice Lily running towards me with the ball at her feet. It was up to me to stop her. It was up to me to put in a crucial tackle and prevent her from running on to goal.

But it felt like all time stood still. Instead of tackling, I simply stood back. Even Lily flashed me a worried gaze as she sped past, easily sliding the ball into the makeshift goal.

'What was that?' the coach screamed at me. 'What were you thinking, Martha?'

I stood there, still frozen, staring at the girls as they looked back at me, confused. I could see Lily moving towards me – her hand reaching out. She was saying something, but I couldn't make out the words.

My body started shaking. I felt a sudden sickness inside of me and it propelled me to move. I had to move. I had to get away.

So I ran.

'Martha!'

I could hear Lily calling behind me. She was running too, but I couldn't let her catch me.

This time, perhaps only once in my life, I was faster.

16

I avoided training after that. I told Mam and Hettie that I had hurt my ankle and they seemed to accept it. After all, they had enough on their plate, rather than worry about me.

The weeks passed, moving us swiftly into November, and with each week that went by, it became easier to stay away. I stayed away from Lily, too. It wasn't that I didn't want to see her – I did. But at the same time, the feelings I had for her were twisting me up inside even more. I wasn't sure I could cope with facing her again. I was certain she thought me so foolish, so silly.

She called at the house a few times, but I made Mam tell her I had a headache or was too tired to go outside. Now that she knew about my dad, I feared that she only wanted to see me out of pity. In some ways that was the was worst thing of all. Mam didn't like lying for me, but she did it. Her and Hettie both assumed we'd had some kind of falling-out. It was easier to make them believe that, than to tell the truth.

What would they think of me if they knew what had really happened? How could they ever understand?

I even tried writing Lily a letter. It was a daft idea really, but I wanted to apologise for saying what I did. The thought that I had ruined our friendship rested heavily with me. I was too ashamed to see her face to face, but I thought I could put my words down in writing.

I only got as far as:

Dear Lily,
I'm sorry

And then the words dried up. I didn't know what else to say.

I really had ruined everything.

Our friendship was over.

I was sitting outside in the yard when Hettie came to fetch me. I had been trying to do some ball practice to take my mind off things, but I quickly found that my heart wasn't it in. Instead, I stood with my back up against the house and stared at the sky.

I remembered the time when me and Lily had

looked up at the clouds and laughed about the faces we could see. It had only been a few months ago, but it felt like years now. How quickly everything could change.

'Ey up...'

I turned at the sound of her voice. Hettie was holding two cups and she handed one to me. 'I was making a brew and I thought you might need one. Mam says you've been sitting with Dad most of the day.'

'Aye,' I replied, gratefully taking the mug. I'd barely drunk anything all day and my throat felt tight and sore. 'He's been sleeping a lot. Not talking at all.'

Hettie perched herself on the doorstep; she gestured for me to join her, and I did. It was a tight fit, our bodies pressed up against the doorframe, but it felt nice. Secure.

'He's getting weaker,' Hettie said softly. 'I caught Mam crying in the kitchen. She thinks just the same. His heart isn't working properly at all.'

A shiver fluttered through my body. 'I don't know, Hettie... I keep hoping...'

'But we have to be realistic too, lass. He's not well, not well at all.' She sipped her tea. 'In all honesty, he hasn't been well for some time. All those years he worked at the docks after his accident. Mam said it was putting great strain on his body.'

I felt myself slump a little. 'I don't want to give up on him.'

'It's not about giving up. It's about facing up to things.' Hettie's voice was stronger now. 'It's what Dad would want. He wouldn't stand to see us moping around like this. He'd want us to do things, to help Mam.'

'But I am helping Mam!'

'I know you are, lass . . . but I mean in other ways.' She sighed. 'Mam doesn't need to keep worrying about you.'

'Is she?'

Hettie nodded sadly. 'This fall-out with Lily, Martha. We can see how sad it's made you. Mam can too. She hates seeing you like this.'

'I'm sad about Dad . . .' I muttered.

'Of course you are, but it's times like these that you need your friends around you.'

I couldn't answer. I missed Lily so much, it was like I was carrying a huge rock inside of me. But could we ever really be friends again? It was all so hopeless.

'I'm sure whatever it was that happened between you, can be put right,' Hettie said. 'You have to have faith.'

'Do you think?' I whispered.

'Aye . . . I do.' She squeezed my hand. 'Good friends will always come back to you in the end.'

We sat together in silence for a while, just comfortable in each other's company. It was so good to have Hettie here, beside me as always.

I wondered fleetingly how long this would last for. When would Hettie or Freddie move on from this house? It wouldn't be long, surely, and then what? Would all the burden of keeping Dad happy, of helping Mam – would that all fall on me?

As if reading my mind, Hettie pulled her arm around me, drawing me closer.

'It's scary, isn't it, lass? All of this,' she whispered. 'I'm scared, too. I go in to talk to Dad and I can barely bring myself to do it. He's not the same.' She paused. 'I wish I were more like you.'

'What do you mean?'

'Well, you seem to handle it better. You know how to comfort Dad. How to cheer him up. You are a natural.'

'Do you really think so?'

'I know so,' Hettie said. 'I wish I could think like you do. You're always the positive one; the sunny girl. Mam and Dad say the same.'

'I don't think I've been that lately, Hettie,' I whispered. 'It's hard being sunny all the time . . .'

'Oh, I understand that. It's been a hard couple of weeks. What with Dad, the team news, Mam worrying about money.'

I sighed. 'I don't even know what I'll do when I leave school. The time is going so fast, and I have no idea. There are so many men looking for work now . . .'

'And men take the priority.'

'I remember the stories you told me about Grace Sibbert and how she was keen to prove to the boys how good you all were.'

'Aye,' Hettie replied. 'Grace was a special one. Without women like Grace, the team may never have been born. She never gave up, you know? I wrote to her recently. I told her the news. I know she's going to be so upset about it all.'

'But what would she say?' I asked. 'What would she do if she was here now?'

Hettie laughed softly. 'Oh, she'd have some words to say, all right! She'd be telling us to fight back. To not take any nonsense. She wouldn't just roll over and accept this.'

'I thought so . . .'

Hettie's hand found mine, she gripped it tight.

'Nowt will happen, lass. The Football Association are likely to get bored of us and move on to other matters. I'm sure they have better things to do. We are probably fretting about nothing.'

'And Dad?'

Hettie was silent for a moment, then she spoke gently. 'He's very sick, Martha. I think we have to face that. We need to be strong for each other. For Mam.'

'But what if I can't be?'

Hettie rested her head against mine. 'You can, lass. You're much stronger than you think.'

17

I don't think I'll ever forget the date. The 5th of December 1921. It was the date that marked the beginning of the end for the Dick, Kerr Girls.

Before then, we were just about coping with life. I was going to school, coming home, helping Mam and seeing to Dad. Hettie and Freddie were working hard, trying to earn some extra money. The days were long and draining, but I made myself press on, forcing a smile on to my face every time I stepped into Dad's room. It didn't matter how sick he looked – or how much his shrunken body scared me – I made myself act cheerful and be the daughter that he needed me to be. Perhaps it was easier in some ways – while I was wearing a mask, playing a part, I didn't have to confront the emotions that tumbled around inside me.

Outside, I could still hear the occasional game of football, but luckily the cold weather kept most of the lads indoors. Hettie told me that Lily had asked after me several times at training, but I pretended that I wasn't bothered by it. I was glad that Lily hadn't visited me again and I ripped up another letter to her that I had started but hadn't finished. It was all too painful. I'd decided she was better off without me.

Hettie kept us all posted on the Dick, Kerr games. She even told Dad about them when he was feeling strong enough. He liked to hear the results. But every time she did, I could feel a hollowness opening up inside of me. I longed to be with the team. I still wanted to be at the games, cheering them on, but my heart couldn't be in two places. It was too shattered; too damaged to do that.

I was with Dad when we heard. He had been a little less tired that day, and was sat propped up by pillows, while I tried to shave his beard. Dad liked to be clean-shaven and Mam said I had a steadier hand than her. I was focusing carefully, sweeping the blade gently over the sharp contours of his face. Had he always been this thin, or was I overthinking everything now?

'You're good at this, Martha. A proper little nurse.'

'Really? Do you think so?'

'Yes . . . I do.' He touched my hand to stop my movement. 'You are a natural.'

'I could do this . . .' I said, my thoughts tumbling together. 'Maybe it's something I could train to do when I've left school?'

'I can't think of anyone more suited.'

'Really?'

'Yes – you are calm, you are kind. You like helping people.' He smiled weakly. 'And you make me feel much better.'

'A nurse . . .' I swirled the blade around the bowl, considering it. 'Maybe I could . . .'

'Well, lass. I don't think it's a bad idea at all.'

I smiled. The more I thought about it, the more I liked the idea. I remembered the wonderful nurses at the Moor Park Hospital who had helped Freddie after his awful war injuries. Freddie still talked now of their kindness and compassion.

A nurse could change someone's life.

'And what about the football? I've not seen you go out and play in ages . . .'

'Well, I can still do that, Dad. In my spare time.'

'Yes, of course – but you need to practise. You haven't been.'

'Well, it's been so cold, and I've got other things to worry about now, haven't I?' I began to sweep his cheek with the blade again, taking extra care around his nose. 'More important things.'

Dad laid a hand on my arm, stopping me. 'You still need time to yourself, lass. Don't waste your days sitting here with me. You love your football. I don't want to stop you doing that, too.'

'It's all right, Dad—'

'No.' His voice was firmer now. 'You have to remember—'

But his speech was broken by the slam of the front door and Hettie's frustrated cry.

'It's over. It's all over. They've finally got us.'

Hettie was in the kitchen, tears of rage framing her eyes. She drew herself a water from the sink and then placed it down in front of her, not even bothering to take a drop. Mam walked over to her and touched her shoulder.

'What is it? Whatever has happened?'

Hettie spun round; her eyes were looking everywhere. She finally settled on me, standing in the doorway, Dad's razor still clutched uselessly in my hand.

'The Football Association have banned us,' she said. 'They've actually gone and done it.'

Mam made Hettie sit at the table and take a few calming breaths. Then, finally, after she had settled herself, Hettie was able to explain properly.

'Mr Frankland heard today. He's so upset, and angry too. Apparently, the Football Association Council met last night. A stuffy group of sixty men, sitting around the table and deciding the future of women's football. They had reports from loads of people, but the reports from the medical professions really dealt us the final blow. Some doctors actually told them that football was a dangerous pursuit for ladies and could run the risk of physical harm.'

'I bet the FA leapt on that,' I muttered.

'Of course they did. It doesn't even make sense. No one questions ladies playing hockey, wielding a great big stick and running around a pitch. How is that any different?'

Mam sighed. 'Well, it's clearly not.'

Hettie sniffed, swiping her nose with her sleeve. 'It doesn't matter anyway. The Association have made their decision. They've declared that it's an unsuitable sport for women, that the money raised in the matches is still not being dealt with appropriately and that complaints have been made to them about women playing.'

'So, what does that mean exactly?' I asked.

'The council declared that any clubs belonging to the Association must now refuse to let us use their pitches for matches. That's any women's football. None of us are allowed to play on FA-owned pitches.'

I shook my head. 'This doesn't sound right, Hettie. Surely they can't do this?'

'They can, and they have,' Hettie replied, her voice still wobbling. 'As of today, women's football has effectively been banned in this country. It's over for us. All of the hard work. All of the money raised, and this is what they do to thank us.' Her fist hit the table. 'It's not fair. It's criminal.'

And it was at that point when she finally burst into tears.

'Will you come with me?'

Hettie was going to Alice Norris's house. A few of the girls would be there, including Lily Parr and Alice Kell. She wanted to talk to them face to face about what had just happened.

I thought of Lily and hesitated.

'I'm not sure they will want me there too, Hettie.'

'Of course they will. And *I* want you there. I might cry again or make a show of myself. I need your support.'

I nodded. How could I refuse? I hated seeing Hettie in such a state. I also hated to think of how upset the girls would be when we told them. It was too devastating.

We were sat outside Alice Norris's house. Lily, Jessie, Flo and Alice Kell were with us. For a while, no one had spoken. The blow of the Football Association's decision was still hanging heavy between us. I sat away from Lily and avoided all eye contact. I still felt so uneasy about what I had caused between us.

Finally, Alice Kell sighed loudly. 'I shall have to say something about this, as captain. I'll make an announcement. I can't stay quiet.'

Flo squeezed her arm. 'Think it over, Ali. Take your time.'

Lily was scowling. 'What is there to say? They've got what they wanted. They wanted to stop us playing. They've won.' She scuffed her feet on the ground in frustration. 'What are we meant to say to that? Well done?'

'There's suggestions that we can still play on Scottish grounds, or in Ireland . . .' Alice Norris said. 'I'm not sure how that will work.'

'How can it?' Lily replied. 'They don't want us to be paid to play. How can we afford to travel all over the place? Most of us still need to work.'

'So, what is the answer?' Flo asked gently. 'It's all such a mess.'

Alice Kell shrugged. 'I don't know, lass, but I'll think of something. I won't remain silent.'

Jessie nodded. 'None of us will. They can't expect us to.'

Alice Kell scowled. 'This isn't over, not by a long shot.' Her gaze drifted off into the distance. Her voice dropped to a whisper. 'It can't be.'

In the distance, we could hear the sound of another football game being played on the street. We heard the shout of a lad's triumph and then laughter.

Yet again, as a team, we were united – but this time it was in grief.

Freddie brought home a copy of the *Lancaster Post.*
He showed it to both Hettie and I in the kitchen,
away from Dad so as not to disturb him. We were
all doing our best to tiptoe around the house as
much as possible. Dad needed as much rest as he
could get.

'Look, Mr Frankland has spoken out about the
ban,' Freddie said, pointing to the page. He spread
the newspaper out on the table so we could both see
and then sat back on the chair.

'Oh, yes, he said he was speaking to the paper,'
Hettie replied. 'Even though he knew it would
do little good.'

I started to read the article. It was quite clear
that Mr Frankland had been struggling to hold
back his disgust. As I read the words, I imagined
his voice saying them out loud, his face heavy
with disappointment. It made my body swell with
rage on his behalf. He had worked so hard to get

the team where it was; it must be so disappointing for him.

> The women's game could continue if organisers of charity matches would provide them with grounds to play on. Dick, Kerr were only paid for expenses for travelling, accommodation and loss of time at work. The girls were in no way paid for playing football.

'God forbid that women be *paid* for playing,' Hettie spat. 'That really would tip our critics over the edge. It's awful that Mr Frankland has to confirm that they aren't, just to shut those idiots up.'

I continued reading.

> Dick, Kerr Ladies Football Club do not think the FA are capable of judging whether the game is harmful or not.

'He's right,' Freddie muttered. 'It's just an excuse. Surely they can't believe that football harms women?'

'Look,' Hettie said, scanning the page. 'He goes on to say how the team has raised around fifty thousand pounds for charity for ex-servicemen and hospitals. If people just realised that, maybe they wouldn't be so quick to judge.'

I turned away from the article. It was almost too sad to continue reading. I hated seeing everything in print. It made it all too final, somehow.

Later still, Alice Kell made a statement of her own. Her words tore through me like sharp briar. It was clear that she was distraught by the decision but in my opinion, she had never sounded so strong and defiant.

> Girls have the right to play football if they desire. We play for the love of the game and are determined to go on. It is absolutely impossible for working girls to afford to leave work and play matches in Scotland, Ireland and up and down the country and be the losers. I cannot see the slightest reason why they should not be recompensed for loss of time.

Hettie grinned when she read Alice's words. It was the first time I had seem her smile for days.

'That's my girl – that's my Alice,' she said, nodding in appreciation. 'This isn't over yet, not by a long chalk.'

Over the next few days, I was amazed to see the waves of support that came the Dick, Kerr Girls' way. It was suddenly quite clear that we were not alone – and many felt, like us, that the Football Association had made a reckless and damaging decision. Ex-football stars came forward, lending their support and stating that women should be allowed to play, just as long as it was against other women.

'After all, we wouldn't like to show the men up,' Hettie muttered.

There were even doctors speaking up in support of the girls, claiming football was no more damaging to women than men. It was as if the country was completely divided in its opinion of whether the girls should be allowed to continue.

Freddie came home with the brightest news.

'It's been reported in the *Lancashire Post* that a Ladies' Football Association has just been formally inaugurated,' he declared.

'What does that mean?' I asked.

'It means that a ladies' version of the FA might

be formed to promote the women's game and donate to charities and deal with the finances, so that no further complaints can be made,' he said. 'We have to hope that this is part of the fight-back.'

'But where will we play?' I asked. 'We are no longer allowed on Football Association pitches.'

Hettie shook her head sadly. 'This is what Mr Frankland is looking into. We can only hope that he finds an answer.'

That was all we could do now.

Hope.

When there was a knock on the door the next day, I ignored it. I felt tired and gloomy and didn't want to talk to anyone. When I heard Lily's voice, my stomach twisted even more. I could still barely stand to see her, let alone speak to her directly. The thought made me wobble inside.

Mam came into the kitchen to find me. 'Your friend is here,' she said. 'She wants you to go out on the bike with her.'

'Oh, Mam, I'm still not feeling up to it. I—'

'Nonsense,' Mam scolded. 'That poor lass keeps knocking and you keep turning her away. I'll not have it.

If you have a problem with her, you need to talk about it properly, rather than skulking around the house like a wounded animal.'

'But, Mam . . .'

'No.' Her voice was firm, but her eyes were kind. She gently squeezed my arm. 'You need to go outside, get some fresh air. What harm will it do?' She paused as her gaze drifted back towards the front door. 'And that poor Lily is desperate to talk to you. She looks upset. Are you really going to be so cruel as to turn her away again?'

I shook my head. No. I couldn't do that to Lily.

Mam was right . . . it was time to face my fears head on.

To begin with, we rode in almost silence. Lily had smiled weakly when I agreed to join her and asked how I was; how Dad was. Her questions were polite and a little awkward, and I answered them in the same tone. It was a relief to mount the bikes and begin to ride. The tension began to ease away a little, as the cool breeze whipped at our faces and the hilly route burnt the muscles in the back of our legs. We rode fast, urgently forcing our bikes forward as if in a race. It was exhilarating.

We took a break at the top of the hill and spent a few minutes just taking in the sights. Lily was standing quite close to me and I knew that she, too, was lost in thought.

I couldn't look at her, I couldn't do anything. I felt rooted in place. Suddenly, every thought and fear seemed to overwhelm me. I thought of Dad back at home struggling to breathe, of Mam cleaning the kitchen with her back to me so that I couldn't see her crying. I thought of Hettie, staring out of the bedroom window, her face tight with disappointment. I thought of the team, the Dick, Kerr Girls, broken and beaten by an unfair and unjust system. I thought of Lily, of the feelings I had for her, swirling inside of me, building up in an uncontrollable wave.

It was all too much. I couldn't keep the tears back. I heard myself gasp and splutter as they escaped from me, and my entire body felt like it was about to crumble.

'Oh, Martha . . .'

Lily rushed to me. She pulled me into her arms, and I found myself burying my head in her chest while she carefully stroked my hair.

'It's all right, lass . . .' she said. 'It's all right. We will get through this, I promise.'

'Do you think?' I sobbed. 'I feel like everything is falling apart. I always try to stay positive, but it's impossible now . . .'

'Things will get better,' she soothed. 'These storm clouds will pass and bring on brighter days.'

'But . . . but . . .' I stuttered, struggling to find the words. 'What about us? I ruined everything. I ruined our friendship with my silly words.'

'You haven't ruined anything,' Lily replied sternly. 'Come on, sit beside me. We need to talk about this.'

Hesitantly, I knelt on the ground beside her. Lily placed her hands in her lap and drew a breath, then she turned to face me, her eyes glinting with tears.

'Martha, it's quite all right to be feeling how you feel. There's nowt wrong with that at all and I'm flattered that you have such feelings towards me . . . but I just don't feel the same. That's not to say that I don't care about you. Or think that you are one of the most wonderful people I've ever met. It's just, to me, you're like a sister, and my dear friend. In many ways, that's just as precious.'

'Is it?' I whispered.

Lily's hand touched my arm. 'Of course it is. It means that you'll always be part of my life and that I still love you, just in a different way.'

I felt my body shudder. My heart felt like a heavy block inside of me.

'I'm stupid . . . so stupid.'

'You're not. You're beautiful and funny and clever.' Lily's voice was rising. 'Anyone would be lucky to have a girlfriend like you.'

'But not you?' I was shaking; I couldn't make my body be still.

'Not me,' she said gently. 'But I'm still here for you, Martha. Always. That is a promise.'

She held out her hand, and I took it. For a while we simply sat there, holding hands. The silence that whipped around us was now gentle and soothing.

'I'm sorry,' I said finally. 'I messed everything up.'

'You did nothing of the sort,' Lily replied. 'Now, shall we have some lunch? My stomach is growling like an angry tiger.'

I laughed as Lily pulled a face at me.

I had my precious friend back, and, just for a while, my worries began to melt away.

The journey home was so much lighter. I felt freer and less troubled by heavy thoughts.

In my daze, I almost shot straight past Freddie,

who was standing outside the front door, frozen like a statue. Instead, I let the bike clatter to the floor and rushed back towards him.

I knew, as soon as I saw his ghost-like expression, what had happened.

I knew, as soon as his bloodshot eyes met mine, what he was about to tell me.

And the remains of my heart splintered into tiny pieces.

It was my turn to see him.

Hettie had just left the room, her face wet with tears, her mouth working words that she couldn't quite say. In the kitchen, Mrs Daniels was making tea for Mam. Mam had barely spoken a word to me. She had been with Dad when he took his last breath. There had been nothing she could do, but she blamed herself, nonetheless.

And now it was my turn.

It was my turn to say goodbye.

I'd never seen a dead body before. Freddie had. In the war, of course. He still had nightmares and cried out at night. Jane at school told us all about the body she once found down at the docks. No one was ever sure if she was telling the truth, but she loved to tell us how grey it was. How lifeless and frightening.

But Dad was not of Freddie's nightmares. Or Jane's horror stories. He was the exact opposite.

As I stood by his bedside, finally I could see a man at rest. The pain was gone from his face. His mouth was relaxed into a slight smile. His eyes were closed. He looked quite beautiful.

Was he dreaming? I wondered dimly if death was one continuous dream. If Dad could enjoy his days running or being out in the sun – no longer worrying.

I leant forward and pressed my lips against his still-warm cheek.

'Goodbye, Dad . . .' I whispered. 'I can't believe . . .'

The words wouldn't come. They choked up inside of me. I felt my legs crumble and I fell to the floor, my hands clutching Dad's covers, but I still felt unable to cry properly. It was like everything was stuck inside of me.

'I can't believe . . .' I whispered. 'I can't believe . . .'

I couldn't believe this was finally the end.

I'd never see my dear dad again.

Later that night, Mam came to find me. I was sat in the bedroom alone, curled up on the bed. I found it hard to move, too hard to be downstairs with the others.

'Lass . . .' She sat down beside me, her hand resting on my shoulder. 'Are you all right?'

'I don't know.' It was an honest answer.

'We knew it was coming, but it's still such a shock.' She took a sharp breath. 'I know how hard it is.'

'It's not fair.'

'He was in great pain, Martha. Great pain. And now he's free.'

But I'm not, I wanted to say. I remained quiet instead.

Mam shuffled next to me. Carefully she placed something on to my lap. It was a small piece of folded paper.

'He knew for some time that this was coming,' she whispered. 'He wrote to all of you. He wanted you to read it. After . . .'

I couldn't look at her. I couldn't touch the letter. The heaviness shifted inside of me.

She squeezed my shoulder. 'Read it, Martha. Please. He wanted you to.'

And then, slowly and quietly, she left the room.

It was much later, hours later, I think, when I finally uncurled the letter and moved to the window to read it. It was short – everyone knew that Dad wasn't much of a writer.

But suddenly it became the most important letter in the world.

My Darling Martha,

You always lit up my life with your smile. You'd be the one I'd call on to cheer us all up. You are the fire in the heart of our family. You helped me so much at the end. Don't let your flame go out.

I may not be alive, but I'm still with you. Never forget that.

I want you to know that I'm so proud of you. I always have been. I always will be, no matter what you decide.

Live your life well, my sweet one. Don't be sad and always remain fearless.

You may not win every fight, but you can win the battle.

Stay strong,
Dad xx

I carefully folded the letter back up and placed it in my pocket, close to me. It was my dad's final gift and I wasn't going to let it go. I would keep it with me for ever.

I slowly returned to the bed, curled up in a ball and finally allowed myself to cry.

20

The week passed in a blur. Dad's funeral was a quick and solemn affair. I could barely bring myself to think about it. Mam was thankful that Dad had paid money into a scheme that meant he didn't end up with a pauper's service and we were able to afford a small plot at the back of the church and a simple wooden cross. She couldn't bear to stay too long after the burial though, and Freddie had to take her home. Hettie and I lingered, unable to tear ourselves away.

'It'll be somewhere to go,' Hettie said. 'When we want to speak to him.'

I stared blankly at the wonky piece of wood. I already knew that my dad wasn't here, in the damp dark earth. Instead, he was with us, in our hearts.

'What did his letter to you say?' I asked her quietly.

Hettie smiled. 'He told me he was proud of me and that he was sorry he didn't support me before . . .' She hesitated, her gaze resting on the grave. 'He told me that the Dick, Kerr Girls deserved to do well and that we mustn't give up.'

'That sounds like Dad.'

Hettie nodded. 'What did he say to you?'

'He said he was proud of me too and that he didn't want my fire to go out,' I replied. 'He told me to live my life well.'

'And you shall.' She smiled.

'I was thinking . . . Dad said I cared for him so well at the end and I enjoyed doing it, too. It felt right. I think that I might want to train to be a nurse, like he suggested.'

'Really?' Hettie turned to me. 'That sounds like a grand idea. Would you still have time for football?'

'I'm sure I will,' I said. 'Although, maybe just for fun. I think I might prefer that. I'm not sure I'm ever going to be as good as you, or the rest of the girls.'

'You are good at football, Marth,' Hettie said softly. 'But I can see you will be a wonderful nurse, too.'

'Well, I will still train with the girls. If it happens, it happens.'

Hettie sighed. 'Aye – we just have to hope that all will be well. At least we have a ground now, thanks to the Dick, Kerr factory providing us with one, so games can go ahead.'

It was a light in an otherwise quite dark tunnel.

We stood for a moment longer. Hettie carefully linked her arm through mine and drew me close. We stood and gazed at Dad's final resting place. I remembered how once he had told me that he hated being still, that he liked to be busy all the time.

At that moment, a butterfly flitted in front of us. It paused on the wooden cross and opened up its wings. It was a wonderful deep-blue colour. Dad's favourite.

'Look . . .' I breathed.

Hettie squeezed me tighter to her.

The butterfly settled for a second or two and then, just as quickly as it had appeared, it flew away again. A bright blue jewel, sparkling in the sky.

It was free.

Christmas was quiet and sombre. We didn't worry too much about presents, but Mam still insisted on making us a good dinner. We sat together afterwards, huddled in the living room. Mam had packed Dad's bed away. She only pulled it out again at night, for her to sleep on. I found myself still staring at the space he had occupied, wondering how things could change so suddenly. Would I ever feel normal again?

'What will you do tomorrow?' Mam asked.

Hettie looked uneasy. 'There is a match at Lively Corner. The girls' first game on their new pitch. After the ban, we are not sure if anyone will come, but I want to go and support them.'

'Of course,' Mam said. 'You should go too, Martha. You need to get outside.'

I hesitated. 'Mam . . . I don't know . . . You need me here, don't you? You don't want to be alone.'

I wasn't sure I was ready to go and watch a game again. It felt too soon, after Dad.

Mam grinned weakly. 'Well, actually, I was thinking of coming too . . .'

Hettie clapped her hands. 'Mam – that would be wonderful! I've always wanted you to come.'

'What's made you change your mind?' I asked gently.

Mam's smile widened. 'It was something your dad said to me on that last morning I sat with him. He took my hand and told me that I shouldn't be sad, that I should treat each day as an adventure and enjoy as much of it as I can.'

'That's beautiful,' Hettie whispered.

'Aye, it is,' Mam nodded. 'And I was thinking, what I would enjoy most would be to spend time with my children. Sharing their love. Being together.'

And so, I stood with Hettie, Freddie and Mam on the grounds of Lively Polly Corner, on a bleak and cold winter's afternoon. Mam was quite excitable about the whole affair and asked no end of questions. She also took much pleasure in telling the spectators close to us that Hettie 'helped to run this team', her son Freddie 'took photographs' and Martha 'was good enough to train with them'.

I don't think I'd ever seen her look so proud.

The Dick, Kerr Girls were about to face the Fleetwood Ladies, and by all accounts were excited to play their first home game. Fleetwood were one of the best teams in the country, so we knew this would be a tight match. Despite the ban, there were still thousands there to watch the girls. It certainly said a lot.

'They are playing this match to raise money for the Clog Fund for Poor Children in the town,' Hettie said, wrapping her arms around her body to keep warm. 'Every penny raised will go to them.'

'I wish the silly critics could see that and appreciate the good they do,' I muttered, feeling the frustration burn within me. Although Lively Corner was a nice enough ground, it was nothing like the standard of Goodison Park or Anfield. It seemed so unfair that the teams had been reduced to this, when all they did was good things for the community.

'Alice Kell has even invited medical professionals here today,' Hettie said, pointing to a small gaggle of spectators in the far corner. 'She wants them to watch the game with their own eyes, to see that there is no risk to women.'

'Let's hope they come to their senses,' Mam said stoutly. 'It's about time someone did!'

The game itself was a tight one, as expected, and although the Dick, Kerr Girls were the superior side, Fleetwood put up a strong fight and the final score was a little unfair to them. Lily was on top form and managed to secure two wonderful goals of her own. Just seeing her celebrate and grin from ear to ear made my heart leap again.

'She is the most wonderful player, isn't she?' Mam whispered to me. 'You're lucky to have her as a friend.'

I smiled. 'Yes. Yes, I am.'

Flo scored the third goal, a lovely sharp volley from outside the box. It looked as though the girls would keep a clean sheet, when Jessie unfortunately made a mistake with a clearance off her own line and knocked the ball back into her own net.

Final score: 3–1.

Mam hugged us all once the final whistle blew. 'What a game,' she breathed. 'It's good to see girls playing this well. I can see now why you love them so much.'

'So, will you come again?' Hettie asked.

Mam's grin was almost as wide as her face. 'You just try and stop me!'

Alice Kell came to speak to us all afterwards. Her cheeks were flushed with excitement.

'Did you hear?' she said. 'One of the doctors I invited has been interviewed. She has just said that she doesn't think football would be any more damaging to a woman than a heavy day of laundry. She said with the right training and support, she cannot see the harm.'

'Oh, Alice, that's great,' Hettie replied.

'I mean – folk might not listen, but it's a start,

right?' Alice said, beaming. 'We are fighting back. We won't stop playing. We won't be told that we can't do this.'

'Good for you,' I said. 'Nor should you.' I thought of Dad's letter to me and recited the words quickly, before I could stop myself. 'You may have lost the fight, but you haven't lost the battle.'

'Exactly!' Alice exclaimed. 'And with all of us, with us all together, we can carry on and make it work. I know it.'

I felt as light as air, and somehow, I swear I heard my Dad's voice softly whispering in my ear.

'That's my girl . . .'

21

We were riding out again. It was a lovely, bright January afternoon, and what better way to spend it than by being in the fresh air. It felt good to be back on my rickety old bike; it even felt like some normality was returning to my life.

As usual, we didn't speak much. We just took in the sights and allowed the silence to fall over us like a comforting blanket.

This was what was perfect about Lily. I could relax. There was no need for mindless chatter or idle gossip.

I could simply be me.

We stopped at our usual resting place, this time perching ourselves on a bench rather than spreading our blanket on the cool grass. Lily, as usual, began tucking into the food she had brought, pulling out sandwiches, biscuits and fruit from her bag and giggling at my perplexed expression.

'You know I love my food,' she said. 'It's my second favourite thing after football!'

I laughed. I was well aware of that fact.

'How are you, lass?' she asked, munching into her sandwich. 'Are you coming to the next training session?'

'I hope to, but I have a meeting with the matron at the hospital later this week,' I said. I could feel the combination of nerviness and excitement building up inside of me. 'She's going to tell me more about the training I can expect there. With any luck, I can start when I finish school next year.'

'You will make a fine nurse,' Lily declared, swiping at her mouth. 'They would be lucky to have you.'

'I hope so.'

'But you need to come to football training too – when you can, of course. The girls miss you. And it's good for you, you know that.'

I nodded. I did. And I wanted to go back. Now that I knew I wanted to explore football more for fun, rather than for anything else, the pressure had lifted.

'I loved playing as a kid,' I said. 'I thought it was all I wanted to do when I was younger, but now I've realised there's other things I want to do with my life, too.'

'Football can still be part of your life. You're in the

Dick, Kerr family now.' Lily smiled. 'That makes you very special indeed.'

'It really does.'

We continued to eat for a few more minutes, watching in wonder as a robin hopped near our feet, searching for crumbs. He was so brave and beautiful. It reminded me of the wonders that still existed so close to hand.

'Do you think everything will be all right now?' I asked. 'I mean, even though you have a ground to play on, it's not the same, is it?'

Lily shrugged. 'I think we just have to wait and see and remain hopeful. Mr Frankland has told us that there is interest elsewhere. Apparently, teams in America would still like us to come out and play there. Can you imagine that?'

I breathed out. No, I couldn't. 'That would be wonderful.'

'I would love to go to America. Just imagine . . .' Lily tilted her head up towards the sky. 'You know, Martha, I really do think that the opportunities are there for us to take – we just have to keep looking for them. This team has so much more to show.'

'I hope so, Lil.'

'Stop hoping, lass,' she said softly. 'And start believing.'

We stayed there for an hour or so, simply enjoying the sights and each other's company. Although I was in no rush to get home, I wasn't afraid, either. Each day was getting slightly easier. We were adjusting to life without Dad. Mam was taking in washing to earn more money and was also spending time with other women in the street, making friends and keeping busy.

Hettie was kept occupied by Mr Frankland, helping him to explore new opportunities and ventures for the club. She was excited by the future.

And Freddie – well, Freddie was doing extremely well at the newspaper. His latest photos had drawn all sorts of acclaim and he was being lined up for a senior post. One that would take him up and down the country. For the first time in forever, he no longer looked like a haunted ghost from the war. He looked like my big brother, ready to take on the world.

And me? Well, I was ready to face whatever came my way. Dad was right. I could do anything with the right attitude. I just needed to be strong. I needed to believe in myself.

I turned to face Lily. Here was probably the most wonderful person I'd ever met. I only hoped I could find a true love like her one day.

'You are going to be remembered, Lily Parr,' I said, finally breaking the silence. 'Mark my words. People will remember you.'

Lily took my hand in hers and she chuckled softly. 'Oh, I don't know about that. I'd quite like my footballing to be remembered. But nowt else.'

'You'll have statues and all sorts.'

'Ah! Don't be daft – of my ugly mug?' She snorted. 'I doubt it.'

'Well – I'll never forget you,' I whispered.

She squeezed my hand. 'You won't need to, you daft apeth. I told you before, I'm here. I'm your friend, always.'

I smiled back, because, in the end, that was what mattered. Friendship. The greatest love of all.

'We have a bright future,' Lily said. 'All of us. Just you wait and see.'

And finally, I truly believed her.

DICK, KERR
GIRLS

THE
PERFECT
SHOT

EVE AINSWORTH

ABOUT THE AUTHOR

Eve Ainsworth is an award-winning author, creative workshop coordinator and public speaker, who draws from her extensive work with teenagers to write authentic, honest and real novels for young people.

Eve is also a passionate football fan and although being born with two left feet, she can often be found on a cold Saturday afternoon cheering on her son from the sidelines.

Eve lives in Crawley, West Sussex with her husband, two young children and slightly crazy dog.

IF YOU LIKE THIS, YOU'LL LOVE . . .

A masterpiece of emotional storytelling.

'A MASTERPIECE OF
EMOTIONAL STORYTELLING.'
ANTHONY McGOWAN

NO
MAN'S
LAND

JOANNA NADIN

How far would you go
to save someone you love?

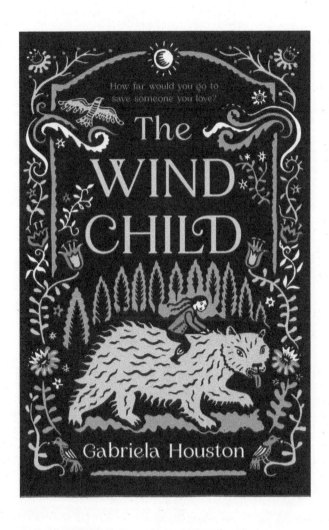

What if you could conjure the clouds?

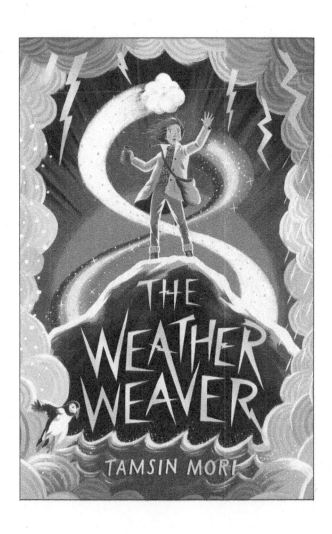

Dare you travel to Inchtinn – where sinister beings stir and tormented souls seek revenge? What if survival relies on facing your greatest fears?

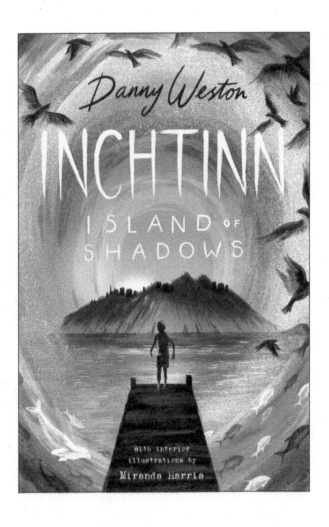

The first book in a gripping fantasy
adventure series from New York Times
bestselling author, A. J. Hartley.

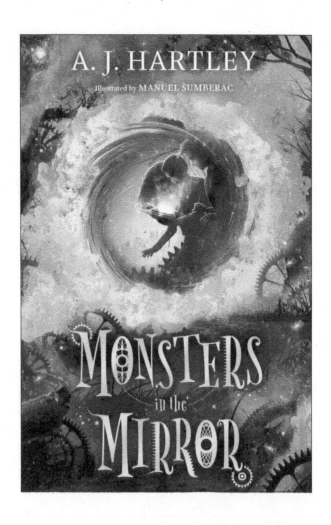

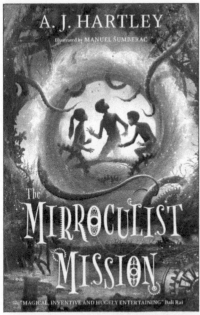

'A wonderfully written, delightful story, full of diverse characters, from a hugely talented author. Highly welcome and recommended'
Bali Rai

'Brilliant, brilliant, brilliant. A. J. Hartley is a true master of the written word'
Christopher Eccleston

The first book in a new electrifying series
from author of *Sky Thieves*, Dan Walker.

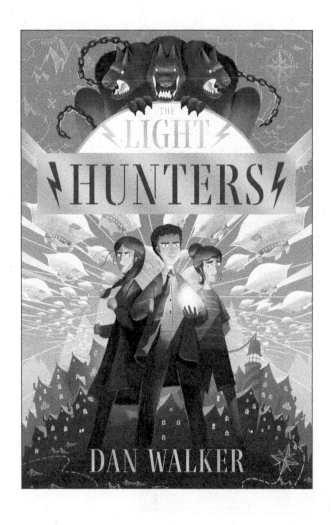

A rollicking medieval romp where laughter
and action abound in equal measure . . .
And where danger lurks around every corner.

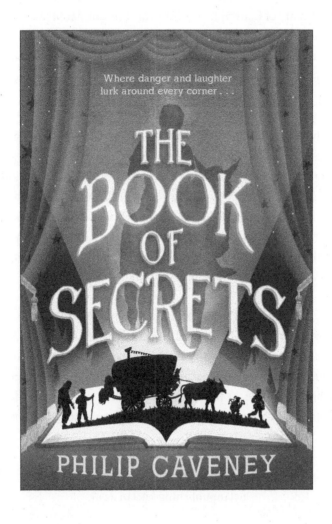

HAVE YOU EVER WONDERED
HOW BOOKS ARE MADE?

UCLan Publishing is an award winning independent publisher specialising in Children's and Young Adult books. Based at The University of Central Lancashire, this Preston-based publisher teaches MA Publishing students how to become industry professionals using the content and resources from its business; students are included at every stage of the publishing process and credited for the work that they contribute.

The business doesn't just help publishing students though. UCLan Publishing has supported the employability and real-life work skills for the University's Illustration, Acting, Translation, Animation, Photography, Film & TV students and many more. This is the beauty of books and stories; they fuel many other creative industries! The MA Publishing students are able to get involved from day one with the business and they acquire a behind the scenes experience of what it is like to work for a such a reputable independent.

The MA course was awarded a Times Higher Award (2018) for Innovation in the Arts and the business, UCLan Publishing, was awarded Best Newcomer at the Independent Publishing Guild (2019) for the ethos of teaching publishing using a commercial publishing house. As the business continues to grow, so too does the student experience upon entering this dynamic Masters course.

www.uclanpublishing.com
www.uclanpublishing.com/courses/
uclanpublishing@uclan.ac.uk